1) Explain time and place with examples
2) Show that the ending does not fit with the theme or plot.
3) Show how the ending fits wi
4) select any example of the u

Kasper in the Glitter

PHILIP RIDLEY

Kasper in the Glitter

illustrated by
Chris Riddell

DUTTON CHILDREN'S BOOKS • NEW YORK

For Ryan—
may you never be tempted
by King Streetwise

P.R.

Library of Congress Cataloging-in-Publication Data
Ridley, Philip.
Kasper in the glitter/Philip Ridley; illustrated by Chris Riddell.
—1st American ed.
p. cm.
Summary: Ten-year-old Kasper encounters a series of fantastic
adventures among the glitter and gloom of the city when he visits it
for the first time.
ISBN 0-525-45799-2 (hc)
[1. Adventure and adventurers—Fiction. 2. Humorous stories.]
I. Riddell, Chris, ill. II. Title. PZ7.R4265Kas 1997
[Fic]—dc21 96-52213 CIP AC

Published in the United States 1997 by Dutton Children's Books,
a member of Penguin Putnam Inc.
375 Hudson Street, New York, New York 10014
Originally published in Great Britain 1994 by Viking U.K., London
Typography by Semadar Megged
Printed in U.S.A.
First American Edition
1 3 5 7 9 10 8 6 4 2

Part 1

KASPER THE SAFE

1

"I'm getting worried now," Kasper mumbled to himself. He looked out the window at the setting sun. "Good heavens, it's hard to concentrate on cooking when I'm this bothered."

Kasper was in the kitchen making a Banoffi pie.

Now—just in case you don't know—Banoffi is one of the most delicious pies ever invented. It's made with sliced bananas, gooey toffee, and topped off with coffee-flavored cream, chocolate granules, and a large dollop of marmalade.

The marmalade, to be honest, is Kasper's own particular addition to the recipe. He says it gives the dish a much needed tang. And he should know. After all, nobody could have made as many Banoffi pies as ten-year-old Kasper Whisky.

Banoffi pie helps cheer Pumpkin up, you see. And as Pumpkin—that's Kasper's mother—needs a lot of cheering up, it follows that Kasper has made a lot of pies.

"You make the best pie in the whole world, honey," Pumpkin often told him.

"Not today I don't!" said Kasper, remembering her words. "All this worry has made me slice the banana too thick and mix the toffee too thin and leave lumps in the cream. And as for the marmalade . . . well, there is none!"

Marmalade was one of the things on Pumpkin's shopping list.

That's where Pumpkin was now: shopping.

And she was late coming back!

"Where can Pumpkin be?" Kasper wondered. "She's never been this late before. But I mustn't get flustered! That won't help! Best keep busy! Let's see . . . the Banoffi pie's finished—all except the dollop of marmalade, of course. I'll put it in the fridge to keep cool. Now what shall I do? I know! I'll clean the sunbeds!"

Now, most houses don't have sunbeds in them, I'm sure you'll agree. But Kasper's house wasn't like most houses. In fact, it wasn't like any other house I've ever seen.

Years ago, you see, Pumpkin had turned the front of the house into a beauty salon. She'd installed not just sunbeds, but hair dryers, couches, and piles of magazines, and called the place SPARKLE PLENTY. There was a big yellow neon sign saying as much above the front door. All day it would flash on and off, and—at night—it would light up the street.

When there was a street to light up, that is.

Because just as the salon was becoming really successful, men in bulldozers came along. For months and months, they knocked down houses and streets. They said they were going to build new ones. But . . . they never did.

They just went away.

Leaving a wasteground with only one thing remaining: the house where Pumpkin and her newly born Kasper lived.

So now you understand why I say it wasn't like any other house I'd ever seen.

Come to think of it, Kasper didn't look like any other boy I'd ever seen, either.

His suit was yellow.

His shirt was lemon yellow.

His bootlace tie: canary yellow.

Kasper was nothing but yellow, yellow, yellow from head to foot.

And I mean that literally, because his hair (which was smoothed flat and hard with a mixture of sugar and water) was golden blond (which is almost yellow), and his shoes (which were very pointed) were mustard yellow.

Yellow was Pumpkin's favorite color.

Most things in the house had been painted yellow. Including the sunbeds, which Kasper was now dusting.

"Perhaps Pumpkin's lost," he said. "Perhaps she'll never come back. . . . Oh, I mustn't think like that! Keep busy! That's the answer!"

So, after cleaning the sunbeds, he dusted the hair dryers.

Then swept the floor.

Then polished the mirrors.

And he was just about to tidy the magazines when he glanced out the window and saw—

"Stars! Good heavens, I'm getting really worried now! If it gets much darker, Pumpkin won't be able to find her way back. I'd best turn the sign on!"

Kasper flicked a switch by the front door, then rushed out into the garden.

The SPARKLE PLENTY sign was flashing, making the house look like a lighthouse in a vast sea of rubble. Kasper looked at the City in the distance.

It was on the other side of the wasteground, the lights in its tall buildings glimmering against the twilight sky. Kasper often wondered what it must be like to live in the City, to have people buzzing around you all day and hear the roar of traffic outside your bedroom window. But he tried not to dwell on it too much. Pumpkin hated the City and got upset every time Kasper talked about it.

In fact, Kasper had never so much as stepped beyond the fence that surrounded his house.

Again, Pumpkin would get upset if he did.

So now Kasper stood in the garden, staring at the City and saying to himself, "I'm getting really, really worried now! Perhaps Pumpkin's been hurt and . . . No! Mustn't think like that. Keep busy! Let's see . . . I'll water the roses!"

The house was surrounded by a forest of roses. There were rose trees in every corner, climbing roses across the side of the house and along the fence, and rosebushes nearly everywhere else.

And the color of the roses?

Yellow, of course.

"Stolen roses!" Kasper gasped. "Here! Five or six roses have been picked. And here! Three or four broken stems. It's the fifth day in a row that roses have gone missing. It must be happening at night. No one could get into the garden during the day without me seeing them. But who? Or what?"

And that's when he heard a voice.

"I think I've broken a fingernail, honey," it said.

"Pumpkin!" cried Kasper. "You're home!"

umpkin sat at the kitchen table. "Could you get me some nail varnish please, honey," she said.

"Certainly," said Kasper, rushing to the salon.

"And mascara, honey!"

"Certainly."

"And hair spray, honey!"

"Certainly."

"And hurry, honey, hurry! I look as ugly as a dishcloth, I'm sure I do! I've never felt less sparkling. And you know how important it is for me to sparkle. Remember my motto: You have to sparkle against the dullness of it all!"

Kasper rushed round the salon collecting the makeup and hair spray, then returned to the kitchen and put everything in Pumpkin's lap.

"Just look at my nail, honey," she moaned, showing Kasper the nail on the middle finger of her right hand. "Carrying those silly shopping bags has broken it. Of course," she added, shooting Kasper a look, "it's all your fault."

"*My* fault!" gasped Kasper. "What did I do?"

"Your shopping list, honey!" Pumpkin explained, painting yellow varnish on her damaged nail. "It was far too long." She glanced at the bags of shopping in the corner. "It's a nightmare carrying that lot all by myself."

Kasper wanted to say that the only reason she had to carry it by herself was because she refused to let him go with her. But he didn't want to upset her any more than she already was, so all he said was, "I'm sorry, Pumpkin." Then added, "Watch out! You're getting varnish all over the table."

"Oh, please clean it up, honey." Pumpkin sighed. "I'm too busy getting myself sparkling."

Pumpkin's hair was blonde and styled in a beehive,

with a rose sticking out of the side. She wore a yellow leather miniskirt, yellow stiletto-heeled shoes, and a yellow silk blouse covered with frills. Pinned to the blouse was a golden brooch in the shape of a rose. This was Pumpkin's favorite object and she always wore it.

"How does my hand look, honey?" she asked, showing Kasper her newly varnished nail.

"Very sparkling," Kasper told her, wiping varnish from the table.

Pumpkin smiled, then started to put on the mascara.

"Watch out!" warned Kasper. "You're flicking mascara on the floor."

"Oh, please clean it up, honey. I'm busy getting sparkling."

Kasper got a dustpan and brush from the cupboard.

"Everything about the City is so ugly," Pumpkin moaned. "It looks ugly, it sounds ugly, and it smells ugly. I bet the smell of the City is in my clothes. I need my rose-water perfume, honey!"

"But I'm cleaning the floor!"

"*Please*, honey!"

With an impatient sigh, Kasper rushed to the salon and got a bottle of rose water. "There!" he said, putting it in Pumpkin's lap.

"Lashes all finished! How do they look, honey?" Pumpkin fluttered her eyelids.

"Very sparkling," Kasper told her.

"The City must be the one place on earth where it's impossible to sparkle," she continued, dabbing perfume on her wrists. "Even someone like me—whose natural instinct is to sparkle—becomes dull." She started to spray her hair. The spray went everywhere, filling the kitchen like a smog.

"You're choking me!" Kasper spluttered.

"Best open a window then, honey," she said, not bothered by the fumes at all.

Kasper opened a window and gulped in the cool night air.

There's the City, he thought. It's hard to imagine it being as ugly as Pumpkin says. All those shining lights. It looks quite beautiful to me—

"How does my beehive look, honey?"

Kasper turned to see Pumpkin's hair glistening with droplets of hair spray. "Very sparkling," he told her.

"Not a hair out of place?"

"Not a single one."

"Now, honey, are you going to look out of that window all night or what? There's shopping to be put away, you know! Honestly, do I have to do everything myself?"

Kasper removed the frozen vegetables from the shopping bags.

"You missed some varnish on the table, honey! Look! There's a large blob of it right there!"

Kasper was beginning to clench his teeth in anger now. Mustn't lose my temper, he thought, cleaning away the varnish. I know—I'll count to ten. That sometimes helps. One, two, three—

"And why's the window open, honey?" Pumpkin continued. "I can feel a draft. Do you want me to catch pneumonia or something?"

Kasper closed the window.

—four, five, six—

"And what about a drink, honey? I go all the way to the City to get your shopping, and then I come home and I don't even get offered a glass of lemonade. Do you want me to die of thirst?"

Kasper got a bottle of fizzy lemonade from the fridge and poured a glass.

—seven, eight—

"Of course," said Pumpkin, sipping the lemonade, "I would have preferred a cool glass of milk, but as you still haven't put the milk in the fridge, it won't be very cool, will it, honey?"

 —nine—

"And what about
something to eat? I
suppose you want
me to starve to death?
Honestly, honey, can't you
do just one little thing
for me—"

 And that's when
Kasper lost his temper!

3

've had enough!"
snapped Kasper. "All you do is boss me around. 'Do this,
honey! Do that, honey!' While you just sit there doing
nothing. Or, rather, you get varnish on the table, mascara
on the floor, make the air so thick with hair spray I can't
breathe." He took a deep breath. "And the only reason
you go by yourself to get the shopping is because you
won't let me go with you! And you know why! Because
you're afraid I'll make a friend—"

And then he stopped.

Pumpkin had started crying. Mascara-black tears were
trickling down her face.

Sob! she went.

Instantly, Kasper was sorry.

Sob!

Good heavens, he thought. I should have kept my big mouth shut.

"Forgive me, pretty Pumpkin," he said. "It's just that . . . well, you were late coming back from shopping. And I was getting really worried. So, I suppose it made me a bit bad tempered."

"I was late because of you, honey!" Pumpkin sobbed.

"Because of me?"

"Of course!" *Sob!* "There was something on your shopping list. . . . " *Sob!* "And the supermarket didn't have it." *Sob!* "So I tried another shop." *Sob!* "And that shop didn't have it." *Sob!* "I tried so many shops I lost count." *Sob!* "But I got it in the end. I thought, 'My honey will be so upset if I don't get his marmalade!' "

"Marmalade!" Kasper gasped. "You went to all that trouble to get some marmalade!"

"Of course I did." *Sob!* "And all the time I was looking, I was getting less and less sparkling." *Sob!* "The wind was blowing my hair and my mascara was smudging." *Sob!* "And then when I get home all you do is shout at me!" *Sob, sob, sob!*

"I'm so sorry, pretty Pumpkin," Kasper said. "Please stop crying. Your cheeks are already black with mascara." Kasper took a handkerchief from his pocket and started dabbing Pumpkin's face.

"I'm sorry if I boss you about," said Pumpkin.

"Don't worry about it," Kasper told her gently. "Now, that's your face all nice and clean. Let's put some more mascara on for you."

Pumpkin opened her eyes very wide so Kasper could put the mascara on her lashes. "You don't want to go to the City and leave me, do you, honey?" she asked.

"Certainly not," Kasper replied. "And there! Your eyelashes are sparkling again."

"Thank you, honey," said Pumpkin, kissing him. "Now give me a hug."

Kasper climbed into her lap. He liked the way her lashes tickled his skin and her warm breath blew down the back of his shirt.

"I love you, honey," Pumpkin said. "You're the most sparkling thing in the universe for me. I'd be lost without my honey."

"I'd be lost without my Pumpkin," said Kasper.

And, suddenly, the two of them jumped up and started dancing with joy. (They often did this when the mood took them.)

They danced around the kitchen table and into the

salon. They danced around the hair dryers and sunbeds and piles of magazines. They danced out of the salon and into the garden. They danced around and around the rose-bushes until Pumpkin got so dizzy she fell to the ground, pulling Kasper with her.

And they lay flat on the grass, looking at the stars and smelling the roses, until they got their breath back.

"You know something, honey," said Pumpkin. "All that dancing has made me quite hungry."

"The pie!" Kasper gasped, sitting up. "Good heavens! I made you a Banoffi pie. Come on, Pumpkin! Let's eat! You'll be glad you went to so much trouble getting that marmalade."

They went back inside the house.

Pumpkin sat at the kitchen table while Kasper got the pie from the fridge, put a large dollop of marmalade on top, then served her a slice. She took a big bite.

"How is it?" asked Kasper.

"Lovely, honey!"

"Banana not too thick?"

"No."

"Toffee not too runny?"

"No."

"Cream not too lumpy?"

"No! It's totally delicious!" *Munch!* "You have some too, honey." *Munch!* "Otherwise I'll end up eating it all and"—*munch!*—"ruin my waistline."

Kasper cut a slice and sat opposite Pumpkin. They ate the whole pie between them, washed down with lemonade.

Afterwards Pumpkin said, "I'm going to bed now, honey. Must get my beauty sleep." She kissed Kasper good-night and started going up the stairs.

On every step she turned, blew Kasper a kiss, and said, "I love you, honey."

As there were nineteen steps, you can imagine how long it took Pumpkin to get up all of them.

Kasper started washing the dirty dishes and putting away the rest of the shopping. He could still smell the hair spray a little, so he opened the window again.

The smell of the garden wafted into the kitchen.

"My roses!" said Kasper to himself. "I wonder if any more will get stolen tonight."

And that's when he had the idea!

Tonight he was going to find out who (or, indeed, what!) was stealing his flowers.

He waited until he heard Pumpkin call out her first "A facial!" of the night (Pumpkin always called "A facial!" when she was asleep, dreaming of the days the beauty salon was full of customers), then he turned off the lights of the house (including the SPARKLE PLENTY sign) and went outside.

"Now, where shall I hide?" Kasper said. "There! The blooms on that bush are as large as dinner plates!"

Very carefully (because the thorns were sharp) Kasper hid behind the bush.

"Not very comfortable here," he muttered. "Good heavens! There's a leaf sticking right up my nose! Perhaps if I lie down I'll be more comfortable. Let's try . . . Yes! A lot better!"

Kasper looked up. "So many stars!" He gasped. "Just look at them all. Millions of worlds. I wonder if there's another boy like me out there. Someone who has no friends. Perhaps, if there is, he might want me to be his friend." Kasper yawned. "We could play together and talk about the best dishwashing liquid to use and"—yawn—"what's the best way to clean windows"—yawn—"somewhere . . . somehow . . . someone must want to be . . . my friend. . . . "

And that's when he fell asleep.

noise!

Kasper's eyes clicked open.

The noise again!

Kasper looked through the rosebush. The garden was very dark. Glancing up, he realized that the moon had disappeared behind some clouds.

The noise again!

Kasper peered through the twigs and into the shadows.

He could just make out a shape. It was on the other side of the garden and near a rosebush. It was about Kasper's size and . . . Yes! Standing on two legs!

Well, at least it's human, Kasper thought, with some relief.

The noise once more!

This time Kasper recognized the sound. The stranger was snapping off roses. Every time another stem broke, Kasper flinched with rage.

Good heavens, he thought. What shall I do? If I tell him to stop, he might slap me round the head—

Another broken stem!

—or kick me on the shin—

Another broken stem!

—or punch me in the nose—

Another broken stem!

"Stop that!" Kasper suddenly found himself crying out, his anger overriding his fear. He clambered from his hiding place.

The stranger yelled and jumped back, falling into the bush and getting caught by the thorns.

"Why are you stealing my roses?" demanded Kasper.

The stranger was struggling too much to answer.

"Tell me!" Kasper said.

And then the moon appeared from behind the clouds and lit the garden.

The stranger was a boy, about twelve years old. He was wearing a black leather biker's jacket, white T-shirt, black jeans, and black pointed boots. His skin was very pale, his eyes very blue, and his black hair styled in a quiff. The roses he had broken off were scattered all around him.

For a few seconds the two boys just stared at each other.

Then the stranger started struggling again. But the more he struggled, the more the thorns dug into his clothes.

"Keep still," Kasper told him. "Otherwise you'll tear your jeans."

The boy stopped moving and glared at Kasper. "You didn't scare me," he said, "so don't think you did."

"I don't."

"Good for you." The boy looked at his jeans. The thorns had ripped through one of the knees. "See what your stupid rosebush has done!"

"You shouldn't be in my garden in the first place."

"You're boring me already." The boy sneered. "Just help me get free, and I'll be on my way."

"I want to know why you're stealing my roses first," Kasper insisted.

"That's my business. Now give me a hand before I blow a fuse. I'm a very short-tempered Heartthrob."

"A short-tempered what?" asked Kasper.

The boy touched his hair. "Just look at this quiff," he said. "What kind of person has a quiff this perfect?"

"I don't know," replied Kasper.

"A Heartthrob!" the boy exclaimed. "And that's what I am. Heartthrob Mink. And, at the moment, I'm a very stuck Heartthrob." He tugged at his clothes again. The sound of ripping could be heard. "These jeans are going to be totally shredded—" Heartthrob stopped speaking as another sound filled the air.

It was Pumpkin calling "A facial! A facial!"

Heartthrob gave Kasper a startled look.

"It's only Pumpkin," Kasper explained. "She usually talks in her sleep, but she never wakes up. Don't be scared."

"Scared? Me? Don't make me laugh! I'm a fearless Heartthrob."

Pumpkin continued to call "A facial!" for a while. Her voice floated round the garden. The two boys stared at each other, listening.

When she'd stopped calling, Heartthrob asked, "She your mum?"

"Absolutely," Kasper replied. "Although she doesn't like me to call her Mum. She says it makes her feel old. So I call her Pumpkin. She's very pretty and—"

"You're boring me again," interrupted Heartthrob. "Just help me get free of this bush, man. My fuse is gonna blow any second!"

Kasper took a step forward. He was so close he could reach out and touch Heartthrob if he wanted to. "My name's Kasper," he said. "Not man."

"I call everybody man," Heartthrob said. "Now stop jabbering and start helping!"

Kasper started to untangle Heartthrob's clothes from the rosebush.

Only five thorns kept him trapped.

"I've looked at a lot of magazines," Kasper told Heartthrob. Four thorns left. "They're full of photographs of Heartthrobs." Three thorns left. "You've got everything they've got." Two thorns. "Except"—the last thorn—"one thing!"

No thorns left.

Heartthrob jumped to his feet, about to run.

"I can give you what you haven't got!" cried Kasper.

Heartthrob peered at Kasper out of the corner of his eye. "And what might that be?" he asked.

"A suntan," Kasper replied. "All the Heartthrobs in the magazines have got suntans."

Heartthrob nodded. "You're spot on there, man," he said. "Sunshine's thin on the ground where I come from."

"I can give you sunshine," Kasper told him. "There's sunbeds inside. I know how to work them."

Heartthrob looked at Kasper thoughtfully for a while. Then he smiled and said, "I've always wanted a suntan."

"Your teeth are very white," Kasper noticed.

"What did I tell you!" Heartthrob smiled even wider. "One hundred percent Heartthrob!"

*H*eartthrob lay on a sunbed. He'd taken off his jacket and jeans and was wearing a pair of special dark glasses to protect his eyes from the light. (He didn't take off his T-shirt, as that would mess up his perfect quiff.)

Kasper sat nearby on a pile of magazines. He was mending the holes in Heartthrob's jeans.

"Getting very hot under here, man," Heartthrob complained, wiping sweat from his forehead. "Hope I'm not going to burn."

"You won't," Kasper assured him. "You can be under there for a few more minutes. I've studied the manual carefully."

"I'm parched, man."

"Would you like something to drink?"

"Wouldn't say no."

Kasper rushed to the kitchen and poured a glass of lemonade, then handed it to Heartthrob.

Heartthrob took a sip and grinned. "Lovely-jubbly," he said, licking his lips.

Kasper sat back down and continued mending the jeans. "Tell me things, Heartthrob," he said.

"What things?"

"About the City," Kasper replied. "I've never been there, you see."

Heartthrob nearly choked on his lemonade. "Never been to the City!" he spluttered. "You're having me on."

"I'm not," Kasper told him. "I've never been anywhere but this house and the garden."

"But . . . you must have seen the City on television."

"We haven't got a television."

"Heard about it on the radio, then."

"We haven't got a radio, either. But I know what televisions and radios look like. I've seen them in magazines."

"You and your magazines!"

"Pumpkin says magazines can teach me everything I need to know."

"Such as?"

"Like . . . well, like how to cook and how to do the housework and . . . oh, yes! . . . how to look your best after an all-night party."

"How many all-night parties you been to, then?"

"Well . . . none," Kasper confessed. Then added, "But when I do, I'll be as fresh as a flower in the morning."

Heartthrob took a deep breath. "Let me get this right, man," he said. "You live all alone out here—"

"I'm not alone! I've got Pumpkin."

"All right, all right! Don't split hairs! And you've never left the house?"

"Certainly not."

"And you've learnt everything you know from magazines?"

"Absolutely. I can cook and do housework better than anyone."

"You do all the cooking and housework?"

"Absolutely."

"What does Pumpkin do, then?"

"She . . . sparkles," Kasper said.

There was a long pause while Heartthrob stared thoughtfully at Kasper. Finally he said, "You're odd, man."

"I'm not odd!" cried Kasper.

"Course you are. Look at you! Cut off from the world and dressed in yellow."

"It's not odd to wear yellow!" said Kasper. "Lots of people wear yellow. I've seen them in—"

"Don't tell me! Magazines!"

"Well, I have!" Kasper was getting upset now. "Anyway, I think *you're* odd!"

"Nothing odd about me, man."

"There certainly is. With your quiff and leather jacket. And calling everyone man. And having such white teeth—"

"All right, all right," said Heartthrob. "Don't fly off the handle. Arguments do my head in. I look odd to you and you look odd to me. Let's just leave it like that and enjoy the sunshine, eh?"

Kasper thought for a while. "Certainly," he said. Then added, "But only if you tell me things."

"About the City?"

"Absolutely!"

Heartthrob sighed. "Oh, anything for a quiet life." Then he took a deep breath. "Right! Let's see! Where to begin? I know, let me ask you something, man! When you look at the City, how many cities do you see?"

"One, of course," replied Kasper.

"One, eh?" grinned Heartthrob. "Well, you're wrong! There're two!"

"Two!" Kasper exclaimed. "What do you mean?"

"Well, the first City is the one you see when you look across the wasteground. The one with the tall buildings full of twinkling lights. The one where people have got somewhere to snuggle up in. This City is called the Glitter." He glanced at Kasper. "With me so far?"

"I think so."

"Then there's the other City," Heartthrob went on. "The City full of people with nowhere to live. This City is called the Gloom."

"The Gloom?" Kasper gasped.

"That's where I come from."

"But . . . what does your mother have to say about that?"

Heartthrob wiped sweat from his forehead and flicked it at the sunbed. It fizzled in the heat and turned to steam. "Don't have a mum," he said.

Suddenly, there was a flapping sound.

A large moth had flown in through an open window and started fluttering round the sunbed.

Quick as a flash, Heartthrob reached out and caught the moth between his finger and thumb. The moth's body was brown and covered with tiny hairs.

Heartthrob grinned mischievously, then thrust the moth at Kasper.

Kasper leaned forward to get a better look.

"You're not afraid of moths!" Heartthrob exclaimed, surprised.

"Why should I be?" Kasper replied. "We get plenty of them out here. Especially when the sunbed's on. They're attracted by the light."

And, as if to prove the point, a few more flew in and started fluttering round the sunbed.

"I'm cooked enough now," said Heartthrob, letting the moth go. "You can turn the sunbed off and shoo the moths out the window, if you like."

While Kasper was getting rid of the moths, Heartthrob went over to a mirror and studied his reflection. "Don't see much of a suntan," he complained.

"It takes a while to come out," Kasper explained. "Here's your jeans."

Kasper had mended Heartthrob's jeans perfectly.

Heartthrob got dressed. "All that sunbathing has made me hungry, man," he said.

"Would you like something to eat?"

"Wouldn't say no."

"How does popcorn sound?"

"Lovely-jubbly."

"And . . . while you're eating it, will you tell me more about the Glitter and the Gloom?"

"You strike a hard bargain, man," said Heartthrob.

Heartthrob sat at the kitchen table, a big bowl of buttery popcorn in front of him.

"Need mustard, man," he said. "Can't eat a morsel without mustard."

Kasper gave him the mustard, then sat opposite. "So . . . you ran away from home, did you?"

"Spot on, man," Heartthrob replied, emptying the jar of mustard on the popcorn.

"But . . . why?"

Heartthrob stared at Kasper. "Listen, man," he said. "All of us in the Gloom have got no home to hang out in for some reason or another. Some, like me, ran away because they wanted to. Some ran away because they had to. Others never had a home to run away from in the first place. Everyone in the Gloom has got their own sob story. And every sob story is different. We don't bore each other with them. I live in the Gloom, and that's all there is to it. With me?"

Kasper nodded. "With you," he said. "But . . . if you haven't got anywhere to . . . hang out in . . . where do you sleep?"

"In a cardboard box," replied Heartthrob.

"A cardboard box!" cried Kasper. "That's terrible."

"In the beginning I didn't even have that," Heartthrob said. "I was on the streets with nothing."

"Weren't you scared?"

"Scared? Me? Don't make me laugh! I'm an optimistic Heartthrob. I knew things would get better."

"So what happened?"

"Well, things got worse, to be honest," Heartthrob said. "It started to rain. Chucking it down it was."

"What did you do?"

"I got wet!" he chuckled. "Ask a stupid question, get a stupid answer, man."

Kasper sighed. "Please be serious," he said.

"I'll try, man. But I'm a naturally humorous Heart-throb. Now, where was I? Rain! That's it! Yeah, it was raining, so I rushed under a bridge to keep dry. Had my quiff to think of."

"What did the bridge look like?" asked Kasper.

"Just a run-of-the-mill bridge, man."

"Describe it to me, I haven't seen many bridges in magazines. It'll help me imagine the story."

"It's not a story," Heartthrob insisted. "I'm telling the truth."

"The truth can still be a story," Kasper told him.

Heartthrob looked at Kasper doubtfully for a while, then said, "The bridge was made of brick, dark brick. And it was a railway bridge. So, in the morning, trains start thundering by overhead. And there was a large poster on the brick wall. A poster of a tropical island: yellow sand, blue sky, palm trees, crystal clear ocean. How's that for a description?"

"Excellent," Kasper said. "So what happened next?"

"Behind the poster was a hole," Heartthrob said. "It led to a stone chamber. So I made that my home. And I learned how to live as one of the Lost."

"The Lost?" Kasper frowned.

"There's two kinds of people, man," Heartthrob explained. "The Lost and the Found."

"What's the difference?"

"You really don't know anything at all, do you?"

"I know different things," Kasper said. "That's all."

"Well, first of all," Heartthrob began, "there's people like you. People who have homes to hang out in. These are called the Found."

"And the Found live in the Glitter?"

"Spot on!"

"And the Lost?"

"The Lost are people like me," Heartthrob replied. "People who have no home to hang out in. We sleep in cardboard boxes."

"And the Lost live in the Gloom."

"You got it!"

Kasper had always thought everyone lived like him: safe with their mums in comfortable homes. He found it hard to imagine what Heartthrob's life must be like.

Heartthrob had finished the popcorn by now, so Kasper put the empty bowl in the sink and started washing it. "I'm still wondering about something," Kasper said.

"Yeah?"

"Why do you want my roses?"

Heartthrob hesitated a moment before replying. "They make someone I know feel at home," he said softly. "Let's just leave it at that, man."

"But how did you know I had a garden full of roses in the first place?" asked Kasper.

Heartthrob took a deep breath. "There I was. In the Gloom one day. When what do I see? A woman. Carrying bags of shopping. With a yellow rose in her hair—"

"Pumpkin!" Kasper cried.

"And I got to wondering if there were any more roses where that one came from. So—"

"You followed her!"

"Spot on, man. I followed her across the Scream—"

"What's the Scream?"

"That's what we call the motorway that surrounds the City."

"So you followed Pumpkin out here, saw all my roses, and . . . just started stealing them."

"That's about it, man."

"And you took them back to this person that roses make feel at home."

"Spot on!"

"Does this person live under the bridge with you?"

"The Arch, yes."

"The Arch?"

"That's what I call the bridge."

"Good heavens," said Kasper, still washing up. "There's so many new words. I'm not sure if I can remember them all."

"It's easy once you get the hang of it," Heartthrob said. "Tell me, what's the Glitter?"

"Where people with homes live."

"The Gloom?"

"Where people with no homes live."

"The Found?"

"People who live in the Glitter."

"The Lost?"

"People who live in the Gloom."

"The Scream?"

"The motorway that surrounds the City."

"The Arch?"

"The bridge where you live."

"Spot on, man! Oh . . . there's one other name you don't know yet."

"And what's that?"

"The Nothing."

"Sounds terrible!" said Kasper. "What's the Nothing?"

"That's what we call this place, man. The waste-ground. Where you live."

The Nothing! thought Kasper. I live in the middle of the Nothing. Good heavens! I'm not sure I like that at all!

Something must have shown in Kasper's face, because Heartthrob smiled and said, "I like you, man."

"I like you, too, Heartthrob," Kasper said, reaching out to hug him.

"Hey, mind your hands," cried Heartthrob, jumping away. "You'll get me all soapy."

"Sorry," Kasper said, drying his hands.

"If you like me," Heartthrob said, "can I see your mother? I mean, Pumpkin?"

"But . . . she's asleep."

"If you let me see her," Heartthrob said, "I'll be your friend."

Kasper thought about it for a while. He knew that, at night, nothing could wake Pumpkin. She would never know if Heartthrob saw her or not. So what harm would it do?

"Certainly," said Kasper at last. "Anything for a friend."

Kasper led Heartthrob up the stairs.

Very gently, Kasper opened Pumpkin's bedroom door, and they went inside.

The room was illuminated by a shaft of moonlight that came through the open window and shone directly on Pumpkin's sleeping face. She was lying on her back, the sheets pulled up to her chin, her long curly hair spread across the pillow like a golden halo.

"Lovely-jubbly," said Heartthrob.

Kasper smiled with pride and nodded.

There was a small Polaroid photograph on the bedside cabinet. It showed Pumpkin and Kasper together, hugging each other and smiling. Pumpkin had taken the photo by holding the camera at arm's length.

Heartthrob picked up the photo and stared at it. "Lovely-jubbly," he said. Then added, "The frame, I mean."

Pumpkin's golden brooch was on the bedside cabinet as well. Heartthrob went to pick it up, but Kasper snatched it away.

"This is Pumpkin's favorite thing," Kasper said, clutching the brooch tight. "It makes her feel sparkling just looking at it."

Suddenly, a moth flew in through the open window and landed on Pumpkin's nose.

"Ha!" Heartthrob laughed, and pointed. "Doesn't look very sparkling with a moth on her nose, does she?"

"Shut up!" snapped Kasper. He rushed over, cupped the moth in his hands, and threw it out of the window. To make sure it didn't fly back in, Kasper shut the window. The moth landed on the glass outside. Its legs made tiny ticking sounds against the surface.

The bedroom door opened!

Kasper turned to see Heartthrob leaving.

"Wait!" called Kasper, rushing after him. "Where are you going?"

"The Gloom calls me," replied Heartthrob, walking swiftly down the stairs.

"But . . . " Kasper couldn't believe Heartthrob was leaving so suddenly. He followed him downstairs and into the kitchen. "But . . ."

"But what, man?" asked Heartthrob, still walking.

"But . . . you haven't got your roses yet!"

"Thought you didn't want me to have any."

They went out into the garden.

"It's different now," Kasper said. "We're friends."

Heartthrob turned to face him.

The roses that Heartthrob had broken off earlier were still scattered on the ground. Kasper picked them up and thrust them into Heartthrob's arms. There were so many that Heartthrob found it difficult to carry them all. When all the flowers had been picked up, Kasper started breaking off some more.

"I'll drop them if you give me too many, man," Heartthrob warned.

But Kasper continued piling them on him.

When Heartthrob's arms were too full to take any more, Kasper started sticking them into his pockets. Finally, he put a rose behind Heartthrob's ear.

"Mind the quiff, man."

Petals were already falling from the blooms, landing on Heartthrob's pointed boots.

"Open the gate for me, man."

Kasper did so, and Heartthrob walked out of the garden and into the Nothing.

"It's very dark out there," Kasper noticed.

"I know my way," Heartthrob said, taking a few steps into the night. "I just go across the Nothing, then cross the Scream, and I'm at the Arch."

"So all that lies between the Nothing and the Arch is the Scream."

"Spot on, man."

Heartthrob continued walking away.

"Will you come back tomorrow night?" asked Kasper.

"Almost probably definitely," replied Heartthrob, his voice getting fainter and fainter.

Kasper peered into the darkness. He could just make out Heartthrob's shape, struggling to hold the roses.

"You're my first friend," Kasper called.

"I'm a very honored Heartthrob."

And then the darkness swallowed him up.

"I have a friend," Kasper said the following morning, as he filled the kettle with water. "I have a friend," he said, as he filled a bowl with cornflakes. "I have a friend," he said, as he put an egg in a saucepan of boiling water.

When he had woken that morning, the first thing he thought of was Heartthrob. His meeting with the boy from the City (or the Gloom) seemed so unreal in the dazzling sunshine that Kasper had been tempted to think it was a dream. But when he had gone downstairs and seen three pieces of mustard-covered popcorn on the kitchen table, he knew that everything had actually happened.

As soon as breakfast was ready (a pot of tea and a boiled egg), he put it on a tray and took it up to Pumpkin.

She was, as always, in a deep sleep, occasionally calling "A facial! A facial!"

Kasper put the tray on the bedside cabinet, then he sat on the edge of the mattress.

"Wake up, Pumpkin," he said loudly.

Pumpkin didn't move.

"Here we go again," said Kasper to himself. "I do wish Pumpkin would stop taking those tablets to help her sleep. They make it so difficult to wake her up."

Kasper shook her shoulder.

"Wake up, Pumpkin," he said.

Still Pumpkin didn't move.

Kasper shook her until the bedsprings started to creak and twang.

"Wake up, Pumpkin!" he yelled.

But Pumpkin merely rolled over and called out "A facial!"

Kasper got up on the bed and started jumping up and down.

He was shouting now. "WAKE UP, PUMPKIN! WAKE UP! WAKE UP!"

I can't keep this up much longer, he thought.

He let out one final, ear-shattering "WAKE UP, PUMP-KIN!"

And that seemed to do it.

Slowly Pumpkin's eyelids fluttered open.

"How do I look, honey?" Pumpkin asked, sitting up.

Kasper put the tray in front of her and poured a cup of tea. "Pretty enough to stop a shooting star," he assured her. "Now, enjoy your breakfast while I go downstairs and get on with the housework."

When Kasper got downstairs, however, he found that he wasn't so keen to do the housework today. He realized that polishing would clean away not only the dust but the signs of Heartthrob as well. Things like his fingerprints would be rubbed away forever.

Kasper didn't want to forget any of the things that Heartthrob had told him the night before. So he got a sheet of paper and sat at the kitchen table to write it all down.

This is what he wrote:

Heartthrob's World

THE LOST—people who have nowhere to live
THE FOUND—people who live in houses
THE GLITTER—parts of the City where the Found live
THE GLOOM—parts of the City where the Lost live
THE SCREAM—motorway surrounding the City
THE ARCH—name of bridge where Heartthrob lives
THE NOTHING—where I live

"So many new things to learn," said Kasper to himself, thoughtfully staring at the sheet of paper. "Pumpkin told me magazines could teach me everything. But she was wrong."

"Honey!" cried Pumpkin. "Come up here! Quickly!"

Kasper rushed up to her bedroom.

Pumpkin was on her hands and knees, looking under the bed. "I can't find my brooch!" she said.

"Your brooch!" cried Kasper.

"I've looked everywhere! Help me, honey! Help me!"

Kasper got on his hands and knees and searched under the wardrobe. But, of course, he knew it would do no good. He knew what had happened to the brooch.

Heartthrob has stolen it! he thought. He must have taken it while I was throwing the moth out the window. That's why he wanted to go so quickly.

"Oh, honey, honey!" Pumpkin threw herself on the bed and started crying. "It's gone! I know it is!" *Sob!* "You know something, I don't really remember taking it off last night." *Sob!* "I probably lost it in the City while I was doing the shopping yesterday. Oh, my sparkling brooch! Gone forever!" *Sob!* "And it's all my fault!"

It's not your fault, Kasper thought. It's my fault. It was me who let Heartthrob into your room. I'm to blame!

"Gone!" *Sob!* "Gone!"

I can't bear to see Pumpkin like this! thought Kasper. But I can't possibly tell her the truth. I need time to think what to do. I'll have to take her mind off the brooch for a while. And it's going to have to be something drastic.

"Pumpkin!" announced Kasper. "I need a facial."

umpkin immediately stopped crying. "A . . . facial?"

"Absolutely," Kasper assured her. "Just look at my skin."

Pumpkin peered at Kasper's face. Then, suddenly, she jumped up and shrieked, "Blackheads!" She whisked Kasper down to the salon and told him to lie on one of the couches. Then she filled a machine with water and flicked a switch. The machine was like a huge kettle and, when the water inside was hot enough, a spout would send steam all over Kasper's face. This would—as Pumpkin explained—open his pores so she could squeeze out the blackheads.

Steaming was the first stage of Pumpkin's facial.

"Clean skin is so important," she said, as if Kasper were a customer. "It helps you sparkle. And sparkling—as I've said many, many times before—is so vital. You know what you have to sparkle against?"

"The dullness of it all," said Kasper.

By now the water in the machine was bubbling away, so Pumpkin aimed the spout at Kasper.

The steam was so hot it turned Kasper's nose bright red. He could feel the redness spread from his nose to his cheeks, then to his lips, chin, and, finally, his forehead.

"It hurts!" he cried.

"Beauty knows no pain," Pumpkin told him.

Kasper gripped the sides of the couch and bit his bottom lip.

I can't believe people

actually paid Pumpkin to do this to them, he thought.

When the steaming was over, Pumpkin turned the machine off and studied Kasper's face through a large magnifying glass. "Quite revolting," she commented. She put the magnifying glass to one side and started squeezing Kasper's nose.

"Ouch!" yelled Kasper.

But Pumpkin only squeezed even harder. "Don't make such a fuss," she told him. "It's the only way to get the blackheads out."

And she squeezed.

"Ouch!"

And squeezed.

"Ouch!"

And squeezed.

"OUCH!"

One particular blackhead (right on the tip of his nose) was so difficult to get out that Pumpkin jumped up onto the couch and sat astride Kasper's chest. She squeezed at the blackhead with all her might.

Good heavens! Kasper thought. I won't have a nose left by the time she's through!

And he was going to tell her to stop, but when he looked up at Pumpkin's face and saw how happy she looked, all he said was one final "Ouch!" and continued to suffer in silence.

After the removal of the blackheads came the face mask.

This was a thick brown cream that, as soon as Pumpkin spread it over his face, started to turn hard as rock.

"Now don't move a muscle," Pumpkin instructed, "otherwise the mask will crack and everything will be ruined."

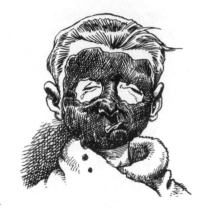

Of course, as soon as he heard that, Kasper wanted to sneeze.

He felt a tickling sensation up his nose so intense that it made his eyes water.

He held his breath.

I must not sneeze! he thought.

But the tickling only got worse.

He clenched his teeth.

I must not sneeze!

Still the tickling got worse and worse.

He could see Pumpkin watching him.

"Don't move now," she warned.

And that's when he sneezed!

Tishoo!

The face mask cracked into a hundred pieces and shot across the room like bits of broken china.

"I told you to keep still!" Pumpkin said angrily. She started to wipe away the remains of the mask from his face. "Do you want to look beautiful or not?" Pumpkin rubbed a thick green slime over his face, then started stroking Kasper's face with a strange-looking object. It was about the size of a pencil, with a silver ball at one end. A current of electricity buzzed through it.

"This will freshen your skin," Pumpkin informed him.

The electricity was so strong it made Kasper's hair stand on end.

Once more he was about to complain (and this time he would have done it, too), but when he went to speak, he realized he couldn't move his lips.

The electricity had made his face muscles go stiff.

Help! Kasper thought.

Pumpkin continued to roll the electric pencil over his face, saying, "So good for the circulation as well."

The electricity was getting stronger and stronger.

Kasper's arms went stiff!

Then his legs!

"It'll make you look ten years younger."

I don't want to look ten years younger, thought Kasper. Ten years ago I was only ten weeks old. Who wants to look ten weeks old?

Kasper started to shake now.

He was shaking so hard that the couch began to rattle beneath him.

It was only when she heard the rattling that Pumpkin turned the electricity off and said, "I hope you enjoyed that."

Kasper was too exhausted to answer.

He didn't fully recover until Pumpkin had removed all the green slime from his face, wiped it dry, then rubbed a soothing moisturizer into his skin.

"All over," Pumpkin declared. "You're as pretty as a picture now."

When Kasper got off the couch and looked in the mirror, he wondered what sort of picture Pumpkin had in mind.

His face was still bright red from the steaming and squeezing.

His hair was sticking up from the electricity.

There were bits of face mask clinging to his eyebrows.

As far as Kasper was concerned, he'd never looked so ugly!

But, of course, he didn't say that to Pumpkin.

In fact, his only comment was, "Thank you, pretty Pumpkin," then he rushed to the bathroom to wash his face and comb his hair.

And now for some housework, he thought. I want to clean away all signs of that thieving Heartthrob. Good heavens! I woke up this morning thinking I had a friend. But I don't. . . . I have an enemy!

one! My sparkling brooch—gone forever. Gone! Gone! Gone!"

All day Pumpkin had been weeping and sighing "Gone!" over and over again. Giving the facial had cheered her up for a while, but it didn't last long. Kasper suggested she take a bubble bath (this usually put her in a good mood), but still she sighed "Gone!"

Now it was evening, and they were sitting at the kitchen table eating an extra-large Banoffi pie.

"How is it?" asked Kasper.

"Gone!"

"Banana not too thick?"

"Gone!"

"Toffee not too runny?"

"Gone!"

"Cream not too lumpy?"

"Gone, gone, gone!"

"You're still sparkling, Pumpkin," Kasper assured her. "Sparkling enough to stop a shooting star."

"Not without my brooch I'm not, honey," insisted Pumpkin. "Without my brooch, a whole universe of stars could shoot right past me without a flicker of hesitation."

"But don't forget your motto, Pumpkin: You have to sparkle against the dullness of it all."

"Without my brooch, I feel the dullness creep up on me by the second, honey. You know how much it meant to me. It reminded me of the days when the salon was full of customers and the sound of bulldozers was a distant rumble. Without it, my sparkle has faded. Dullness, here I come."

Good heavens! thought Kasper. I've never heard Pumpkin speak like this before. I've got to do something.

"Gone! And all because of me! I lost it doing the shopping. Lost a large part of my sparkle! Gone! Gone! Gone!"

"No, Pumpkin," said Kasper. "It's not gone!"

"It's . . . not, honey?"

"Absolutely not! I remember now. You definitely had it on when you got back from shopping!"

"I . . . did?"

"Certainly!"

"Then where is it, honey?"

"It . . . it must have fallen off when we were doing all that dancing last night. Yes! That's it! So it's in the house or garden somewhere."

Pumpkin's eyes were very wide. "Oh, honey . . . you think so?"

"Absolutely! Now why don't you go to bed and leave me to find the brooch for you. I'll search all through the night if need be. I'll move furniture and search the rosebushes. It'll be a lot of hard, dirty work. You don't want to be around for that. And, in the morning, the brooch will be on your bedside cabinet, sparkling just as bright as ever, and the dullness will disappear and you'll stop the first shooting star that comes along."

"Oh, honey! You promise?"

"I promise."

Pumpkin jumped to her feet and kissed Kasper. "I feel better already," she said.

Pumpkin went to bed (after her usual blowing-kisses-and-I-love-you routine on every step, of course) and Kasper sat in the kitchen, waiting for her first "A facial!" of the night.

Of course, he knew he wouldn't find the brooch in the house or the garden.

But he made up his mind about something.

He knew what he had to do.

"A facial!"

Kasper got a candle from the kitchen cupboard.

"A facial!"

He lit the candle.

"A facial!"

He went out into the garden.

It was very dark now.

A moth hovered round the candle flame.

Kasper saw the track of rose petals that Heartthrob had left the night before.

The trail that led across the Nothing.

And across the Scream.

And right to the Arch.

The trail that would lead to Heartthrob.

And the brooch!

"I promise you, Pumpkin," he said, "I *will* get your brooch back. You *will* sparkle again."

Then, for the first time in his life, Kasper opened the garden gate.

And stepped into the Nothing.

Part 2

KASPER THE LOST

11

'm getting nervous now," Kasper mumbled to himself. He hadn't started feeling nervous until he was halfway across the Nothing. Up until then, all he had felt was anger. He wanted to look Heartthrob in the eyes and say, "You're a thief, and I want Pumpkin's brooch back." But, as the lights of the City became bigger and brighter (and the Sparkle Plenty house became distant and dimmer), Kasper's anger was replaced by fear.

He imagined Pumpkin asleep in bed and—for a second—wanted to go back and be comforted by the sound of her calling "A facial!"

But he knew he had to keep going forward!

Forward to the City!

Kasper said, "Heartthrob told me he lived under a bridge called the Arch. All that lies between the Nothing and the Arch is a motorway. The Scream. Now if I can just get to the Scream, I should be able to look across and see the Arch and then I'll—"

A cool gust of air swirled round Kasper.

The candle flame flickered violently.

"That's all I need," Kasper muttered. "To be left in the dark."

And then he realized . . .

He wasn't in the dark anymore!

The electric light from the City was so close it was almost as bright as daylight: an orange glow that made Kasper feel a little safer.

A few more steps and Kasper was standing on the edge of the Scream.

The motorway was like a flat, gray river.

On the opposite side he could see a bridge.

"The Arch!" exclaimed Kasper. "There it is!"

His heart was beating very fast.

He started to walk across the Scream.

It was so much easier walking on the smooth tar after the broken terrain of the Nothing.

Vroom!

The ground started to shake.

Vrooom!!

The sound got louder and louder.

Suddenly a car appeared out of nowhere.

It whizzed past Kasper.

He jumped out of the way.

Only to find himself narrowly missing another car.

Vroooom!!! went the engine.

Beep! went the horn.

Kasper leaped again.

But when he landed, another car seemed to be aiming straight for him.

Kasper screamed and started running.

The turnpike was full of cars now. Cars of all shapes and sizes: flat cars, long cars, cars so new they gleamed like jewels, cars with rust and peeling paint. And all of them, no matter what shape or size, seemed to be heading straight for Kasper.

Vroom!

Beep!

Some of the cars had to swerve to miss him. Their tires went *Screech!* against the tar.

Kasper was spinning from place to place.

Vroom!

Beep!

Screech!

Kasper dropped his candle. It rolled under a particularly large car and got squashed flat as paper.

I'll never get home without it, Kasper thought.

And he would have worried about it longer were it not for a truck heading straight for him.

The headlights were so bright they hurt Kasper's eyes.

He started running.

The truck swerved to miss him.

Screeech!

Something fell from the back of the truck.

Kasper couldn't see what it was. Mainly because his eyes were still bleary from the headlights, but also because—at that moment—he tripped up a curb and fell over.

He lay there for a moment, gasping for breath.

He suspected that if he'd fallen up a curb, he must be on the other side of the motorway.

He felt the ground beneath him.

Pavement, not tar.

I've crossed the Scream! he thought.

Gradually, he got his breath back, and his vision cleared.

He sat up.

Bananas were all around him.

They must have fallen off the back of the truck, he thought.

He got to his feet and looked around him.

All he could see were dark streets and alleyways.

He'd run so far avoiding the traffic that now there was nothing to tell him where he was.

No Arch.

No rose petals.

Nothing.

"I'm lost," said Kasper to himself.

"Oh, we're all lost," said a voice behind him. "Are these bananas yours?"

Kasper turned to see a boy holding a large wicker shopping basket.

"Er . . . no, they're not mine," Kasper told him. "They fell off the back of a lorry."

"Gracious me, what luck!" the boy said gleefully.

He started picking up the bananas and putting them in his basket. "I've got a pie to make, you see. And bananas are one of the main ingredients." When the basket was full, he looked up at Kasper. "I'm Jingo Fleetwood, by the way," he said, holding out his hand.

"Kasper Whisky," Kasper told him, shaking hands.

Jingo was short and had a round face with small, dark eyes. His hair was long, parted in the middle, and looked very greasy. He was wearing black shoes, baggy trousers (rolled at the bottom to accommodate his short legs), white shirt with winged collar, white bow tie, and black tailed jacket. Because Jingo was so short, the tails of his jacket trailed across the ground behind him, getting very dirty.

"A pleasure to meet you, Master Kasper." Jingo peered at Kasper a little closer. "If you'll permit me," he said, taking a clothes brush from his pocket, "you're a little dusty from your fall." And he proceeded to brush Kasper's clothes till all the dirt was gone. "There you are," he said, standing back to admire his work. "Clean as a whistle, if I say so myself."

"Thank you," said Kasper.

"Is there anything else I can clean for you while I'm here?"

"I don't think so."

"Then I'll be on my way. As I told you, I've got a pie to make." Jingo tried to lift the basket, but it was far too heavy. "Gracious me!" he muttered. "I seem to have overdone it in the banana department." He tried to lift the basket again, but without success. "I've got to get the ingredients back," he said breathlessly. "I'm making the pie for a very special person, you see. And if he doesn't get it, he'll . . . be in a"—still trying to lift it—"very yucky mood!"

Kasper couldn't bear to see the boy struggle. "Why don't I carry it for you?" he offered.

"You'll . . . carry it?" Jingo's eyes were wide with surprise.

"Certainly."

"But . . . no one helps me."

"Why shouldn't I help you?" Kasper said. "I've got nothing else to do."

After all, he thought, I don't know where the Arch is. And, without something to light the way, I can't get back across the Nothing until morning.

"A million thanks," Jingo said, bowing slightly.

Kasper picked up the basket. "You're very welcome."

"This way, if you please, Master Kasper," said Jingo. He led Kasper into a long and gloomy alleyway.

Their footsteps echoed around them.

Now that Jingo didn't have the basket to carry, he wasn't quite sure what to do with his hands. To keep them occupied, he picked up his dirty jacket tails, muttered "Gracious me!" then brushed them clean. When they were clean, he let them fall back to the ground, whereupon they soon got dirty again, so he picked them up once more, muttered another "Gracious me!" and brushed them all over again.

Kasper watched Jingo in amazement for a while, then looked round the alleyway.

The City doesn't look very sparkling, thought Kasper. All I can see at the moment are leaking drainpipes, broken windows, and piles of rubbish. And this alleyway smells revolting. It needs a good dose of bleach and disinfectant.

"And now, Master Kasper," began Jingo, his voice bubbling with excitement, "it's my turn to surprise you."

"It is?" said Kasper.

"Have you any idea who I'm going to cook the pie for?"

"None at all."

"Master Kasper," he said "you are holding the ingredients that will make the favorite pie of . . . " And here he took a deep breath so he could say it loudly and with pride, "The King."

"The King?" said Kasper. "The King of what?"

"The King of the Gloom, of course," Jingo replied. "KING STREETWISE!"

And his voice echoed up and down the alley.

"STREETWISE . . . TREETWISE . . . REETWISE . . . EETWISE . . . TWISE . . . WISE . . . ISE . . . SSSSS."

*I*t was the most wonderful name Kasper had ever heard.

"I didn't know the Gloom had a king, Jingo," he said.

"Didn't know!" exclaimed Jingo, coming to a halt. "Everyone in the Gloom knows King Streetwise! And *I*, Jingo, am his personal butler!"

"But . . . I've only just arrived in the Gloom," Kasper explained, stopping and putting the basket on the ground. "So there's still a lot I don't know. Please tell me about King Streetwise. What's he like, Jingo?"

Jingo took a deep breath, then said, "Everything about the King is golden."

"His hair?" asked Kasper.

"Golden."

"His clothes?"

"Golden."

"His shoes?"

"Golden, golden, golden," said Jingo. "He blazes through the night like . . . like a comet!"

"A comet!" Kasper gasped.

"But the most golden thing about him is his friend-ship, Master Kasper," Jingo told him. "Because his friend-ship is so pure and precious. Once you're his friend, you'll do anything for him."

"Oh, Jingo." Kasper sighed. "I want a friend like that!"

"Then King Streetwise is the one for you!"

"Do you think he'll like me?"

"No doubt about it, Master Kasper. And, who knows, he might even say yum, and pat your head."

"I'd do anything to have him pat my head!" said Kasper, breathlessly. "I'll do his housework—"

"I do that, I'm afraid."

"His cooking, then! I can cook anything yellow!"

"That's a coincidence, Master Kasper. The King's favorite pie is very, very yellow."

"Really?" said Kasper. "What's the pie called?"

"Oh, you wouldn't know of it, Master Kasper," Jingo told him. "It's not a very well known pie. It's made of bananas and toffee and—"

"Topped off with coffee-flavored cream and granules of chocolate!" interrupted Kasper excitedly.

"Well . . . yes!"

"It's Banoffi pie, Jingo! Tell me it is! Banoffi pie!"

"I'm quite speechless, Master Kasper. But, yes, you're right. Banoffi pie it is."

"I know how to make the best Banoffi pie in the whole world."

"You do?"

"Certainly! I've made hundreds . . . no, thousands! Millions! Please let me come back with you and cook one for the King. I want him to say yum. I want him to pat my head. I want him . . . to be my friend."

Jingo looked at Kasper thoughtfully. "I don't know," he said. "Cooking for the King is my job usually. I am his personal butler, after all. I don't want to become worthless in his eyes. But, on the other hand, I must admit I'm not very good at making Banoffi pie. I haven't made a pie yet that's made him say yum."

"I'll make him say yum, Jingo. I've got a special ingredient I add to the pie that makes it impossible not to say yum."

"What special ingredient?"

"Marmalade! It gives the dish a much needed tang! Have you ever put a dollop of marmalade on one of your pies?"

"Never."

"That's why the King's never said yum. Have you got any marmalade?"

"Back in my kitchen I have."

"Then please let me cook a Banoffi pie for the King, Jingo!" pleaded Kasper. "He'll pat me on the head for cooking it and pat you on the head for letting me cook it."

"In that case," said Jingo smiling, "to the Palace!"

"The Palace?"

"Where else would you find a king? Come on! This way!"

Jingo rushed out of the alley.

Kasper picked up the basket and followed him. . . .

L ights!

Lights everywhere!

Flashing lights, neon lights, multicolored lights.

Kasper was so taken aback by the brilliance of it all that he just stared and stared.

Lights in shop windows.

Traffic lights.

Yes! Cars!

Hundreds of them.

Roaring up and down the main road.

And the noise!

Screeching tires.

Honking horns.

Music blaring.

And people!

Hundreds of them. Thousands. All kinds of people in all shapes and sizes. All dressed differently. And all of them laughing and talking and giggling and shouting.

The sights and sounds of it all were making Kasper feel quite dizzy.

Jingo came up and tugged at his sleeve. "Don't lag behind, Master Kasper," he said.

"Wh . . . where are we?" asked Kasper, looking all round him.

"This is the biggest street in the Glitter," explained Jingo, brushing dirt from his jacket tails again. "It's always full of people. They come here to shop and drink and eat and see films and . . . well, spend lots of money. Now, are you feeling all right? You look a little queasy."

"I'm fine," said Kasper. And although he was still feeling dizzy, he followed Jingo.

People pushed past them.

The lights kept flashing.

And now there was something else—

Smells!

"What's that?" asked Kasper, sniffing.

Jingo sniffed. "Hamburgers!"

"Smells wonderful," said Kasper. Then smelled something else. "What's that?"

"Pizza."

"It all smells so good, Jingo. And looks good, too. You know, someone once told me the City looks and sounds and smells ugly. But it doesn't. It's . . . it's . . ."

Again Kasper was looking all around him.

On either side of the street were shops. The windows were full of all sorts of things. And everything gleamed like treasure.

The lights from the windows were so bright that they made the pavement gleam as if it had been polished.

" . . . wonderful." Kasper sighed.

One shopwindow was full of televisions. There must have been hundreds of them. And all of them had the same image on their screens: a rocket taking off. The rocket was like a huge white finger pointing at the sky.

"Wonderful!"

Another shopwindow was full of toys. There were models of airplanes, trains, and cars. There were dolls with blue hair and robots with ray guns. There were space-ships hanging from the ceiling and plastic dinosaurs across the floor. One dinosaur seemed to be looking right past Kasper and out into the street, as if yearning for escape.

"Wonderful!"

"Master Kasper! Please keep up with me!"

"Oh . . . I'm sorry, Jingo! I'll be right . . . there. . . ."

But, suddenly, everything was spinning around Kasper.

Flashing lights!

Music!

Rockets!

Dinosaurs!

Hamburgers!

And Kasper collapsed to the pavement, his heart pounding.

"Master Kasper!" cried Jingo. "What's wrong?"

Jingo knelt beside him, loosened Kasper's collar, then took a handkerchief from his pocket and flapped it in front of Kasper's face to give him some air.

Gradually, Kasper started to feel a little better.

"I'm sorry, Jingo," he said. "Everything was too much for me all of a sudden. I feel fine now." Then he looked around him.

People in the street just walked straight past them. Some actually walked over them, as if Kasper and Jingo didn't exist.

"Tell me, Jingo," said Kasper. "Why hasn't anyone asked us what's wrong?"

"Oh, you'll get used to it, Master Kasper," said Jingo, helping Kasper to his feet. "You see, you're one of the Lost now. And the Found make out that they can't see the Lost. To them we're invisible."

"Invisible?" Kasper gasped.

Jingo nodded, then indicated the shopping basket (luckily nothing had fallen out when Kasper had collapsed). "Can you still manage that, Master Kasper?"

"Certainly."

"Then let's get a move on. We're leaving this street now anyway. Come on."

Jingo turned a corner and went into a dark side street.

Kasper picked up the basket and followed him.

"I can't wait to get to the Palace," Jingo went on. "While you're cooking, I'll do some dusting. I love dusting things. Do you know what my idea of perfect happiness is?"

"What?"

"A huge house full of dust and me armed with a feather duster. I would dust it from top to bottom, then start all over again."

Jingo turned the corner into an even darker street.

Then round a corner into an alleyway.

And all the time it was getting darker and darker.

"It's a strange thing, the City," Kasper commented. "One minute it's all fizzy, and the next it's not fizzy at all."

"I agree, Master Kasper," said Jingo. "Fizziness is a fickle thing."

They turned another corner.

"There!" exclaimed Jingo, pointing.

They were standing at one end of a long street.

On either side were empty houses. Some of them were half demolished, revealing rooms inside: walls covered with peeling wallpaper, framed photographs with cracked glass, and, in some cases, a rotten armchair or sofa. All the houses, whether partially demolished or not, had gardens full of bricks and rubbish.

At the end of the street was an old, disused church with a very tall spire.

The church had obviously been abandoned for a long time, because the bushes around it had been left to grow wild, surrounding it like a forest. A path had been cleared through this tangled mass of twigs and branches. It led to the wooden door of the building.

"The Palace!" announced Jingo.

*M*ost of the Palace's stained-glass windows were cracked or smashed. The brickwork was also damaged, with whole areas crumbling or missing altogether.

"Isn't it beautiful?" asked Jingo.

"Oh . . . certainly," Kasper murmured. Although he wasn't sure *beautiful* was quite the word he'd have used.

As they walked down the path leading to the large wooden door, Kasper looked at the overgrown bushes on either side.

Wait a minute, he thought. I'm sure these are rose-bushes. So where are the flowers?

And he peered closer to get a better look.

Only to see . . .

A pair of eyes staring back at him!

Kasper let out a yell, dropped the shopping basket (bananas went everywhere), and jumped back, falling into some bushes. Thorns entangled his yellow suit.

"Gracious me!" Jingo exclaimed. "What's wrong now, Master Kasper? You're dropping that basket more than you're holding it."

Kasper pointed. "Someone's there!" he cried.

"Show yourself!" demanded Jingo firmly.

A figure stepped out from behind the bush.

It was a boy, about twice as tall as Kasper and very, very thin.

The boy had long black hair and pale skin. His clothes—black jeans, black T-shirt, and black denim jacket—were full of holes and very frayed. He was holding a pair of scissors in one hand and a yellow rose in the other.

"It's only Master Skinnybones," Jingo said. "He's one of the Argonauts."

"What are the Argonauts?" asked Kasper.

"The Argonauts are the King's soldiers."

"You're not an Argonaut, are you, Jingo?"

"Gracious me, no, Master Kasper. I told you, I'm just the King's personal butler. You can always tell the Argonauts by their glorious golden helmets."

Kasper looked at what Skinnybones was wearing on his head. It appeared to be made of tin cans, most of which had been crushed flat, then welded together and painted gold.

But it didn't look much like a helmet to Kasper.

More like a metal wedding cake, he thought.

"Nice to meet you, Skinnybones."

"A rose!" Skinnybones exclaimed, ignoring Kasper and holding the flower in the air. "I knew I could smell one!" And he sniffed a few times as if to prove the point.

Jingo started to help Kasper untangle himself from the bush. "If you'll permit me," he said, carefully tugging at a thorn. Then he looked up at Skinnybones and added, "This is Master Kasper. He's going to cook—"

"Another stink!" Skinnybones interrupted. He sniffed the air a few times, then stepped over to Kasper and sniffed again. "You stink of something."

"What?" asked Kasper.

Skinnybones sniffed. "I'm not sure." *Sniff, sniff.* Then, "Furniture polish! You smell of furniture polish. Am I right?"

"Possibly."

"No 'possibly' about it. You've touched furniture polish within the past twenty-four hours. Don't deny it!"

"Well . . . all right," admitted Kasper, "I have."

"I knew it!" exclaimed Skinnybones. "You can't fool this nose of mine. It can sniff out any stink there is to sniff. Wait a minute. I can smell something else now." *Sniff, sniff.* "Bleach. Am I right?"

"Absolutely," said Kasper softly.

"You stink of lots of clean stinks. I'm not used to that. Confused me at first, squire."

"My name's not squire," insisted Kasper. "It's Kasper."

"Oh, I call everyone squire," Skinnybones told him, then looked at Jingo. "Don't I, squire?"

"Indeed you do, Master Skinnybones," said Jingo, trying to untangle the remaining thorns from Kasper's sleeve. "Oh please keep still, Master Kasper."

"Sorry, Jingo." (Kasper had been trying to sniff himself.) "It's just that I never realized I smelt of cleaning products before."

"Just ignore Master Skinnybones, Master Kasper. That nose of his can smell things other people could never smell."

"I can sniff out any stink . . . " Skinnybones began.

"Why don't you do something useful!" snapped Jingo. "Pick some bananas up."

"Not my job, squire. My job is cutting off roses." And he snipped the scissors in the air.

Snip—snip!

"What do you mean your job is cutting off roses?" asked Kasper.

"King Streetwise doesn't like roses," Skinnybones said. "He doesn't like the look of them, he doesn't like the smell of them, and he doesn't like the feel of them. When he sees a rose he yells 'Yuck!' at the top of his voice. Now, all the bushes 'round the Palace are rosebushes. And it's my job to cut the roses off. With these here scissors!"

Snip—snip!

"And what—what do you do with them then?" asked Kasper, putting the last banana in the basket.

"Frazzle them, squire."

"Frazzle them?"

"That's right," said Skinnybones, grinning. "I put them in the oven and burn them to a frazzle."

"But that's terrible!" gasped Kasper. "You can't burn roses! They're too . . . too . . . " He was so shocked that, for a while, he couldn't speak properly. Finally he managed, "They're too beautiful."

"The King doesn't think so. You see this rose I'm holding?"

Kasper nodded.

"Soon it'll be nothing but ash!" teased Skinnybones, grinning even wider.

"No!" cried Kasper.

"Its petals will sizzle!"

"No!"

"Its stalk will crackle!"

"No!"

"Its leaves will—"

"No!" Kasper jumped up and tried to snatch the flower from Skinnybones. "You mustn't burn roses! I won't let you!"

Skinnybones lifted the rose out of Kasper's reach. And as he was so much taller, there was little chance of Kasper getting it.

"It's got to frazzle, squire!"

"Give me . . . give me!" Kasper was getting quite breathless now.

"Really, Master Kasper," said Jingo. "Please stop this. Master Skinnybones has got to do his job. If the King sees a rose, he'll give Master Skinnybones a black eye."

Kasper stopped jumping and looked at Jingo. "He will?" he asked.

Jingo nodded.

"You don't want me to get a black eye, do you, squire?" asked Skinnybones.

"Certainly not, but—"

"Then it's frazzle time for the rose."

Kasper calmed down. The thought of a burning rose saddened him, but he didn't want Skinnybones to get hurt either.

Kasper picked the basket up and looked at Jingo. "I'd best start cooking," he said. "That'll take my mind off frazzling roses."

Jingo opened the door to the Palace.

"After you, Master Kasper," he said.

andles!

That was the first thing Kasper saw when he entered the Palace.

Hundreds of candles.

Candles illuminating everything with a gentle, flickering light.

And wooden pews.

Or, rather, piles of broken wood that used to be wooden pews. An aisle divided the piles of wood in two, and at the end of the aisle was a huge chair made out of tin cans. It twinkled gold in the candlelight.

Jingo noticed Kasper staring at the chair.

"That's the Throne," Jingo explained. "Only King Streetwise is allowed to sit in it."

Suddenly, a figure jumped out from behind the Throne and started running down the aisle towards them.

It was a boy with long, curly black hair and the largest ears Kasper had ever seen. They stuck out from the sides of his head like handles on a jug. His clothes were nothing but rags and, like Skinnybones, he was wearing a golden helmet.

"A moth!" he cried, coming to a halt in front of them. "There's a moth in the Palace. I heard it flapping somewhere." He cupped his hands around his ears to hear better. "I've got to get rid of it."

"This is Master Poodlecut," whispered Jingo to Kasper. "Another Argonaut."

"Hello, Poodlecut," Kasper said. "Why have you got to get rid of a moth?"

"Because King Streetwise doesn't like them," Poodlecut explained. "He doesn't like the look of them, he doesn't like the sound of them, and he doesn't like the feel of them. When he sees a moth, he yells 'YUCK' at the top of his voice. It's my job to make sure the Palace is a moth-free zone. And there's one here now. I just know it, old bean."

"My name's Kasper," Kasper insisted, "not old bean."

"Oh, I call everyone old bean," said Poodlecut. He looked at Skinnybones and asked, "Don't I, old bean?"

"You do, squire," came the reply.

"I'm here to cook—" began Kasper.

"Shush!" Poodlecut interrupted. "I've got to listen for the moth."

They all stood in silence for a while.

Suddenly, a strange gurgling sound filled the air.

Poodlecut looked round nervously. "What's that?" he asked. "Is that the moth?"

"No, squire," chuckled Skinnybones. "It's my stomach. All I can smell is bananas, and they're making me hungry—"

"Shush!" went Poodlecut again. "How can I hear the moth's flapping wings with you jabbering away? You should be helping me."

"Not my job, squire. My job's getting rid of roses, not moths—"

Another strange gurgling sound filled the air.

"What's that?" asked Poodlecut, nervously looking around. "Is *that* the moth?"

"I do apologize, Master Poodlecut," said Jingo. "That was *my* stomach this time. I must be getting hungry, too."

"This is impossible!" complained Poodlecut, stamping his foot. "How am I supposed to hear the moth above the din of your rumbling stomachs. Wait! I can hear it! Flapping wings! Yes, yes. My radar ears are picking them up. There it is!" Poodlecut pointed.

A moth was flying round a candle flame.

Poodlecut chased after it.

Good heavens! thought Kasper. Don't say he's going to frazzle a moth! That would be terrible! I can't let it happen!

"Stop!" Kasper found himself shouting. "Moths are harmless!"

Kasper rushed after Poodlecut.

"What are you doing, Master Kasper?"

"Stop it, squire! Let him do his job!"

"Moths are harmless!" cried Kasper again.

Poodlecut had just cupped the moth in his hands, when Kasper grabbed him around the legs.

Poodlecut fell to the floor.

"Gracious me, Master Kasper!"

"Let go of that moth!" yelled Kasper angrily. "Let go now!"

"But the King will give me a black eye if I don't—" began Poodlecut.

"I don't care! I will not allow you to frazzle a moth!"

"Frazzle!" Poodlecut gasped, keeping hold of the moth for all he was worth. "I'm not going to frazzle it, old bean. I'm going to shoo it out the window."

Kasper froze for a moment, then let go of Poodlecut's legs. "I . . . I feel very stupid all of a sudden . . . " he said. He got to his feet, then helped Poodlecut up. "Good heavens, I've never lost my temper like that before. What a strange feeling that was. I couldn't control what I was doing. Sorry, Poodlecut."

"Don't mention it, old bean." Poodlecut went over to a broken window and shooed the moth outside.

"Gracious me, Master Kasper," said Jingo, taking the brush from his pocket and brushing Kasper's jacket. "You do have a habit of falling over. There! Spick-and-span again. And I sincerely hope you're not going to cause any more trouble. Skinnybones has to get rid of roses. And Poodlecut has to get rid of moths. You may not agree with it, but it's what goes on here and you'll have to go along with it."

"Certainly," said Kasper. "It's just that . . . well, there've been so many surprises since I came to the City."

And the surprises were far from over. . . .

Bang!

11

Something was bashing against the door of the Palace.

Bang!

Kasper jumped.

Bang!

The door nudged open a little.

Bang!

The door opened wider.

Bang!

A baby's pram started inching its way into the Palace.

Bang!

More of the pram became visible.

Bang!

The pram was old and rusty—

Bang!

—with peeling paint and broken wheels.

Bang!

It was full of old tin cans and—

Bang!

—bones!

"Bones!" Kasper gasped.

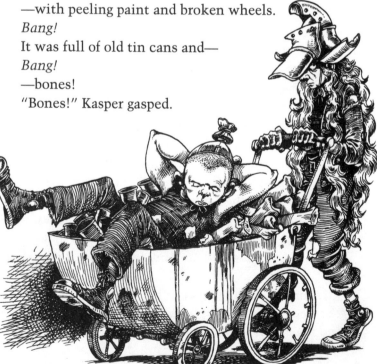

The pram was completely in the Palace now.

It was being pushed by a tall boy, also wearing a golden helmet. He had huge, bloodshot eyes and the longest, waviest hair Kasper had ever seen. It came from under the helmet and reached the boy's knees.

On top of the bones in the pram was another boy.

He was wearing a golden helmet and had muscular arms and legs. There seemed to be tattoos on each arm but, because of the angle he was sleeping at, Kasper couldn't see what they were. Unlike the others, this boy had very short hair.

"Why didn't you help me?" said the wavy-haired boy in a high-pitched voice, looking accusingly at Skinnybones and Poodlecut. "Didn't you hear me struggling to open the door?"

"Not my job, squire."

"Not my job either, old bean."

The boy clenched his fists. His knuckles made popping noises.

Kasper winced and said, "Ouch," instinctively.

"I'm an artist," the boy announced. "It shouldn't be my job to struggle with stupid doors while Philistines like you just stand and watch." His eyes came to rest on Kasper. "What uncool clothes you're wearing."

"Do you think so?" asked Kasper.

"Of course I do," the boy insisted, flicking hair from his eyes. "They're the uncoolest color I've ever seen. What is it? Custard?"

"Certainly not," Kasper said. "It's yellow."

"It might be yellow to you," sneered the boy. "But to me it's custard through and through. Why are you here anyway, chief?"

"To cook Banoffi pie for the King," replied Kasper. "And my name's Kasper. Not chief."

"I call everyone chief," the boy said. Then looked at Skinnybones and Poodlecut. "Don't I, chiefs?"

"You do, squire."

"You do, old bean."

"And as for your hair," the boy went on, popping his knuckles, "not only is it the uncoolest style I've ever seen, it's the uncoolest color, too."

"It's blond," Kasper told him.

"It might be blond to you," sneered the boy. "But to me—once again—it's custard through and through. And look at your shoes, chief! Uncool! And look at your tie! Uncool! And as for your suit! Uncool—"

"This is Master Fingerpoppin," Jingo interrupted, introducing the wavy-haired boy to Kasper. "He doesn't mean to be rude."

"I do!" Fingerpoppin swished his hair from side to side. "An artist has a right to be rude when he sees uncool things. And, believe me, you"—he pointed at Kasper—"are uncool."

"Fingerpoppin makes the golden helmets!" Jingo went on. "He also made the Throne. He makes everything out of rubbish—"

"No such thing as rubbish!" exclaimed Fingerpoppin, curling a strand of hair round his fingers. (*Pop* went a knuckle.) "Just masterpieces waiting to happen. And I don't make things out of any kind of rubbish. Just old tin cans."

Kasper looked in the pram. Some of the cans still had bits of food inside. (Kasper could clearly see half a peach and a sardine.) But there were also the bones.

Bones gleaming in the flickering candlelight.

What were they for?

Fingerpoppin saw Kasper's puzzled expression. "The bones are not mine, chief," he said. "The bones are Knucklehead's here." He flicked the ear of the sleeping boy.

The boy called out "Woof!" in his sleep.

"What does he want bones for?" asked Kasper.

"To feed the dogs," explained Fingerpoppin.

"What dogs?"

Jingo answered this time. "The dogs that pull the King's Chariot, Master Kasper," he said.

"The *cool* Chariot!" cried Fingerpoppin. "The Chariot I made with these hands." And he held his hands out in front of him and wriggled the fingers proudly.

Pop—pop—pop went the knuckles.

"Stop boasting, squire," complained Skinnybones.

"At least I've got something to boast about, chief," retorted Fingerpoppin. "Making masterpieces is a cool job, not uncool like getting rid of roses or moths."

"Nothing uncool with getting rid of roses, squire."

"Nothing uncool with getting rid of moths, old bean."

"They're totally uncool jobs, chiefs."

And, suddenly, Skinnybones, Poodlecut, and Fingerpoppin were all arguing.

Their voices echoed around the Palace.

"Oh, do stop shouting," pleaded Jingo.

But their voices were getting louder and louder.

"My job is artistic, squire."

"So is mine, chief."

"Nonsense, old bean!"

And then a new voice boomed through the Palace.

"YUCK!" it went.

Immediately, the argument stopped.

Skinnybones, Poodlecut, and Fingerpoppin stood very still and stared nervously at each other.

Even Knucklehead, who had remained asleep throughout the arguing, jumped awake and started trembling.

A few bones fell off the pram and clattered to the floor. Jingo instinctively started picking them up.

"YUCK!" boomed the voice again.

Jingo dropped the bones in fright.

The voice was coming from a doorway on the far side of the Palace. Through it, a wooden staircase could be seen leading up.

It must be King Streetwise, thought Kasper. He sounds very angry. And look at the Argonauts. They're so scared. Come to think of it, I'm scared, too, and I don't even know why.

"YUCK!" went the voice again.

"Perhaps he's smelled that rose, chief," suggested Fingerpoppin, pointing at the flower still held by Skinnybones.

"Nonsense, squire," said Skinnybones (although the thought obviously unnerved him). "Perhaps he found some dust."

"Gracious me, no!" insisted Jingo, nervously dusting his jacket tails again. "The Palace is as clean as a whistle."

And they continued to speculate until the voice boomed, "MOTH!"

Poodlecut went very pale. "Another moth," he said softly. "If we hadn't been arguing, I would have heard it fluttering—"

"POODLECUT!" roared the voice.

Immediately, Fingerpoppin grabbed hold of the pram and pushed it down the aisle. "Must get going, chiefs," he said. "Masterpieces to make!" Both he and Knucklehead disappeared through a doorway.

"Must get going, squires," said Skinnybones. "Roses to frazzle." And he ran away so fast Kasper didn't even see where he went.

Poodlecut faced Kasper and Jingo. He looked very scared. Kasper felt sorry for him but didn't know what to say.

"POODLECUT!" boomed the voice again.

All the candles in the Palace flickered.

"I best go," said Poodlecut, his bottom lip trembling.

"Gracious me, yes, Master Poodlecut."

"Good luck," was all Kasper could say.

Slowly, Poodlecut walked across the Palace and up the wooden staircase that led to the steeple.

There was a slight pause.

"What will King Streetwise do to Poodlecut?" asked Kasper.

"Give him a black eye, I suppose," Jingo replied.

"But that's terrible."

Jingo grabbed a nearby candle and held it in the air. "That's nothing," he said. "If his yucky mood continues, he's likely to give us all black eyes. The only thing that might put the King in a yummy mood—and save us all from black eyes—is if you make a delicious Banoffi pie."

Good heavens, thought Kasper. I've never cooked under such pressure before.

Jingo walked towards a staircase that led down.

"Pick up the basket and follow me if you please, Master Kasper," he said. "Time to cook!"

As the staircase had no banister to hold on to (and as the only light came from Jingo's candle), Kasper kept as close to Jingo as he could.

"Be careful there," instructed Jingo, pointing to a step with a large hole in it. "And the next one—here!—that's missing altogether."

Kasper put his hand on Jingo's shoulder to keep balance.

"Don't worry, Master Kasper," Jingo said. "You'll soon get used to the dark."

"I'm not sure I want to get used to it."

"But don't you like candles?"

"Sometimes."

"Like when?"

"Well . . . like when I cook a special yellow dinner for Pumpkin."

"And Pumpkin is . . . ?"

"My mother."

Jingo came to an abrupt halt and stared at Kasper. His small, beady eyes gleamed in the candlelight.

"A word of advice, Master Kasper," he said. "If you'll permit me, of course. Don't mention mothers or fathers or homes to King Streetwise."

"No?"

"No. You're one of the Lost now. Things like that don't exist for us. Now, come on, follow me."

They walked down the remaining steps in silence.

As Kasper trod on the final step, he gasped out loud.

He'd seen a face!

"Pretty, eh?" remarked Jingo, holding the candle close so Kasper could get a better look.

It was a statue of a young child. Its face was smiling, and it had very large eyes. But the most surprising thing about the statue was that it had wings.

"What is it?" asked Kasper.

"An angel," Jingo told him.

"An angel," Kasper repeated. He touched the face of the statue. It felt cold and smooth. A spider crawled across the angel's lips.

"Haven't you ever seen one before?" asked Jingo.

Kasper shook his head. "Not in all my years of looking in magazines. Tell me, Jingo, do they really exist?"

"I don't think so," Jingo said.

Kasper sighed sadly and brushed the spider from the angel.

"Come on," Jingo said. "I'll show you where the Argonauts sleep."

Jingo led Kasper down a corridor. It was made of stone and smelled very damp. He stopped outside a doorway and asked Kasper to look inside.

Kasper saw a large room.

There were five mattresses on the floor.

On each mattress was a pillow and a blanket.

"Do you sleep here as well?" asked Kasper.

"No," replied Jingo. "I sleep in the kitchen."

"Does King Streetwise sleep here?"

"Gracious me, no. The King sleeps in the steeple."

"And have I met all the Argonauts?" asked Kasper.

"Every one," Jingo assured him.

"But . . . there are five mattresses," commented Kasper. "And Skinnybones, Poodlecut, Fingerpoppin, and Knucklehead make only four."

"That's right," Jingo said, turning away. "Now down here"—he led Kasper to another room—"this is where the Argonauts eat."

In the middle of the room was a wooden table surrounded by five chairs. On the table were five plates, five knives, five forks, five spoons, five cups, and five saucers.

"Five of everything again," commented Kasper.

"That's right," said Jingo. He led Kasper to another room. "This is where the Argonauts wash."

In this room were five tin baths, five bars of soap, five flannels, five toothbrushes, and five towels.

"But, why should there be five of everything if—" began Kasper.

"Please don't ask me about that," Jingo said, turning away. "Now I'll show you the kitchen."

But Kasper wasn't interested in the kitchen.

He wanted to know why there were five of everything.

I don't understand this at all, thought Kasper. If there are only four Argonauts, why are there five mattresses and five dinner plates and five—

Kasper gasped out loud as he entered the kitchen.

The kitchen was a vast stone chamber, illuminated by hundreds of candles. In the middle was a wooden table and, against the far wall, an oven.

But not a normal kind of oven.

This oven was old and large and made out of iron. There was a grille at the front through which a fire could be seen blazing. Many pipes ran away from the oven (some going along the walls, others up through the ceiling), and all of them made hissing and rumbling noises.

But it wasn't the gigantic oven that made Kasper gasp.

Nor the hissing and rumbling noises.

Nor the hundreds of candles. (After all, he was used to those by now.)

It was the dogs.

Two of them.

One on each side of the oven.

They're Dobermans, thought Kasper. I've seen photographs of them in magazines.

Both had hard, sharp, yellow fangs and piercing red eyes.

And both were snarling at Kasper. . . .

on't move!" warned Jingo.

Kasper didn't need telling. He was too scared to move even if he wanted to.

"Gracious me!" muttered Jingo, standing very still. "I've told Knucklehead a million times not to let the dogs in the kitchen."

"Are they . . . dangerous?" asked Kasper, barely moving his lips.

"Not if you keep very, very still. The last time this happened, I had to stay still for nearly three hours."

"Three hours!" exclaimed Kasper. (Or as near exclamation as he could get without moving his lips.)

Sweat started to trickle down Kasper's face.

And arms.

He felt his shirt sticking to him.

His hands became moist.

And that's when the basket started to slip through his fingers. . . .

Good heavens, thought Kasper. The dogs are sure to attack if I drop the basket.

The dogs seemed to sense Kasper's anxiety. They stared at him, eyes blazing. Their snarling got louder. Their lips curled back to reveal just how long and vicious their sharp teeth were.

Kasper tried to grip the basket tighter. But still it slipped.

The dogs' eyes blazed.

Their snarling got even louder.

The basket slipped further.

The dogs took a step towards him. . . .

More slipping!

More snarling!

Another step.

"What's wrong?" asked Jingo out of the corner of his mouth.

"The basket is slipping," Kasper said.

The dogs' snarling turned to growling.

"Gracious me!" was all Jingo could say.

Kasper was clinging on to the basket by his fingertips now.

Slipping.

Growling.

Another step.

Good heavens! thought Kasper.

I'm going to be eaten by dogs.

Slipping.

Growling.

Another step.

And then . . .

The basket crashed onto the floor!

The dogs ran at Kasper.

"HELP!" he cried.

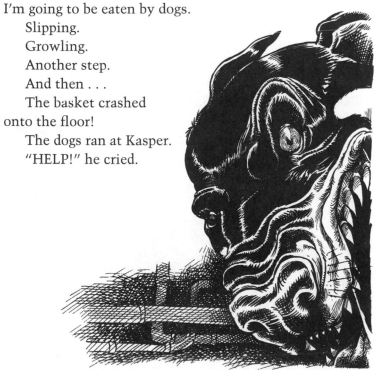

OOF!" went a voice.

The dogs stopped in their tracks.

Knucklehead had entered the kitchen. He was holding the bones that had been in the pram.

Slowly, Knucklehead went over to the dogs and said "Woof!" once again. This time in a gentler voice.

The dogs went back to their places by the oven.

Knucklehead divided the bones between them, then uttered three *woof*s in quick succession, and the dogs started to eat.

"Gracious me, Master Knucklehead," said Jingo, sighing

with relief. "I know they like the warm oven, but I wish you wouldn't leave them down here alone."

Knucklehead sat between the dogs and stroked them lovingly. He looked up at Jingo and grinned. Kasper could see that his teeth were as yellow as the dogs', and that most of them were either chipped or cracked.

"Everything's safe now, Master Kasper," Jingo said, putting the shopping basket on the table.

The dogs looked so different now. Like two puppies. As they ate, Knucklehead whispered gentle *woofs* into their ears.

"What are the dogs' names?" Kasper asked Knucklehead.

Knucklehead just glared at him and said, "Woof!"

"Knucklehead rarely talks to anyone except the dogs, Master Kasper," Jingo explained. "Now, forget about him and start cooking." He got the ingredients for the pie (plus a mixing bowl, spoons, forks, and anything else he thought Kasper might need) and put them on the table.

"Oh . . . certainly," said Kasper, going to the table.

"And while you're doing that," Jingo said, "I'm going to do some dusting." He grabbed a feather duster from the wall and swished it in the air. "I'm sure there's something somewhere that needs to be cleaned up." He rushed out of the kitchen.

Kasper started to prepare the pie.

He was halfway through mixing the piecrust base, when . . .

"Moonglow," said Knucklehead softly.

Kasper looked up and saw that Knucklehead was patting one of the dogs on the head. "This is Moonglow," he told Kasper. Then he patted the other dog and said, "This is Stardust."

"So you *can* talk!" Kasper exclaimed.

"Course I can talk!" Knucklehead retorted. "Don't want to talk most of the time, that's all. Most human things are not worth the effort, matey."

"My name's Kasper," Kasper said. "Not matey."

"I call everyone matey," Knucklehead said. "When I bother to call them anything at all, that is."

"Why don't you think people are worth talking to?" Kasper asked.

"Cos I prefer dogs," Knucklehead replied. And hugged the two beside him. "If I had my way, I'd live in a world of dogs. There'd be dog doctors and dog teachers and dog astronauts. What good are humans anyway? They can't bring a stick back if you throw it, and they haven't got a tail to wag. If I got lost, these dogs would follow my trail, sniffing me out by my scent until they found me. Can you do that, matey?"

"Not that I know of," Kasper had to admit, flattening the piecrust into a pan and starting to peel the bananas.

Knucklehead wrestled playfully with the two dogs. They barked excitedly and he woofed back.

"In my dreams," Knucklehead said, "there are no human beings—woof!—just dogs. And all the dogs look after each other—woof!—and they bark at the sun and howl at the moon and look after their puppies." He lay on the floor, breathless from wrestling with the animals.

The dogs licked his face.

Kasper spread sliced banana over the piecrust. "What are those tattoos on your arms?" he asked Knucklehead.

"Hearts," Knucklehead replied, getting to his feet and displaying his arms. There was a tattoo of a heart on each one. "One for my Moonglow and one for my Stardust."

The dogs were jumping up at Knucklehead and barking. He playfully pushed them aside.

"Doesn't it scare you?" asked Kasper, pouring toffee over the bananas.

"What, matey?"

"Loving something that might be dangerous."

"Nothing's dangerous if you hug it the right way," replied Knucklehead.

Kasper spread the cream over the toffee and sprinkled chocolate granules over the cream. These were the final stages of making the pie except for the marmalade, so

Kasper was being especially careful. He knew that presentation is very important in cooking. And as this was a pie fit for a king, he wanted it to be as neat as possible.

Kasper was so engrossed that, at first, he didn't realize Skinnybones had entered the kitchen. It was only when he heard sniffing that he looked up and saw him.

"That smells tasty, squire," Skinnybones said, indicating the nearly complete Banoffi pie. (He was still holding the yellow rose in one hand and the scissors in the other.) "Hope it's good enough to make King Streetwise say yum!" He walked over to the oven and opened the grille. "If it's not, we'll all have black eyes by morning."

Kasper was just about to say he hoped it would be, too, when Skinnybones hurled the rose in the oven's flames.

"No!" cried Kasper, and rushed over. He instinctively tried to save the burning rose, but the intense heat drove him back. He watched the flames crinkle and scorch the beautiful flower until there was nothing left except ash.

"Now, don't make another scene, squire," said Skinnybones. "It's my job. You know that. It has to be done."

"Certainly," sighed Kasper.

"Now, do your job and finish the pie," said Skinnybones. The dogs started sniffing at his feet. He pushed them away.

"Woof!" said Knucklehead angrily.

"But they stink of bones, squire!"

"Woof, woof!"

And they would have
continued arguing were
it not for Poodlecut
walking in.

Poodlecut was trembling all over, and his left eye was swollen and already turning black.

"The King is in a very yucky mood," he said. He touched his sore eye and winced. "I knew there was a moth. But all you old beans were making so much noise I couldn't hear it."

"Don't blame me—woof!" said Knucklehead. "I was—woof!—asleep."

"And I didn't say a word," insisted Kasper.

"Well, I just hope your pie is good enough, old bean," said Poodlecut, glaring at Kasper with his one good eye. "Otherwise we'll all have—"

". . . black eyes by morning," Kasper finished for him. "I know."

The next second Fingerpoppin strolled into the kitchen.

"That looks cool, chief," Fingerpoppin remarked, pointing at the pie. (*Pop* went a knuckle.) "And that"—pointing at Poodlecut's ever-blackening eye—"looks uncool!"

"It feels uncool, old bean," whined Poodlecut, then added, "What's that noise? It's not another moth, is it?"

"Not to worry, Master Poodlecut," said Jingo, entering, "just me flicking my feather duster." He started to dust the table. "How's the pie coming along, Master Kasper?"

"Just one more thing left to do," replied Kasper, grabbing the jar of marmalade.

"Your special ingredient, Master Kasper."

"Absolutely, Jingo." Kasper took a big spoonful of marmalade and put it on the pie. "There!" he said triumphantly. "A Banoffi pie fit for a king."

"I sincerely hope so, Master Kasper. Otherwise—"

"Black eyes, squire."

"Black eyes, old bean."

"Black eyes, chief."

"Woof, matey."

"Good heavens," said Kasper. "I know my pie's good . . . but really . . . I . . . I . . . " His voice trailed away.

Jingo took the brush from his pocket. "If you'll permit me, Master Kasper," he said. "A little sugar on your suit." He brushed the jacket clean. "And you want to look your best for the King." He stepped back to admire his work. "Good as new, if I say so myself," he said, smiling. He handed Kasper a candle. "You'll need this," he said.

"But won't you be coming with me?" Kasper asked.

"Gracious me, no," replied Jingo, shaking his head. "This is your job."

Kasper gripped the pie in one hand and the candle in the other.

"Good luck, squire."

"Good luck, old bean."

"Good luck, chief."

"Woof, matey."

"Good luck, Master Kasper."

"To the King!" said Kasper nervously.

21

The stairs leading up into the steeple were made of wood and very rickety. Kasper had to tread carefully. He didn't have Jingo to point out the dangerous steps this time. And with the pie in one hand and the candle in the other, he couldn't hold on to anything.

The stone walls on either side gleamed and smelled of furniture polish.

Jingo's obviously been doing some cleaning, Kasper thought.

As he climbed higher and higher, he heard a voice coming from the top.

"Yuck, yuck, yuck," it muttered.

Kasper clutched the pie tighter. The last thing he wanted to do was drop it. He imagined the mess it would make tumbling down the stairs behind him, splattering bananas and cream all over the stone walls. The thought made him shudder.

He continued to climb.

The last few steps creaked loudly.

But louder still was the voice muttering, "Yuck, yuck, yuck."

With a deep breath, Kasper entered the belfry.

A cool breeze swirled around him and blew out the candle.

Kasper looked round.

Through the openings in the belfry, he could see the gleaming lights of the nighttime City, like an ocean of shimmering stars.

A shaft of moonlight illuminated where Kasper stood. Beside him, on the floor, was a bronze bell. It was as tall as Kasper and had a hole at the top.

"Yuck, yuck, yuck," muttered the voice.

It came from the darkest corner.

Kasper took a step forward. He wanted to speak, but when he opened his mouth, nothing came out. Fear had frozen his throat. So he just stood there, clutching the pie for all he was worth, and gaping.

"Well—hey there!—moonlit dude," purred the King from the darkness. "Is that my Banoffi pie?"

"Y . . . y . . . yes," Kasper managed.

Kasper could see something gleaming in the dark. A twinkle of gold. He put the candle down so he could hold the pie with both hands.

"Why don't you just hold that pie out, moonlit dude," demanded the King.

Kasper did as he was asked.

A hand came out of the shadows. It was very pale and had large, golden rings on every finger. Slowly, a finger dipped into the pie, then went back into the darkness.

Kasper's heart was beating so hard, it sounded like running

footsteps in his skull. He listened to the King slurping at the pie-covered finger.

Please like it, thought Kasper. I don't want to get a black eye. Please say—

"YUM!" exclaimed the King.

King Streetwise stepped out of the shadows.

And Kasper saw . . .

Gold!

Gold everywhere!

The King glowed and blazed with golden sequins and rhinestones. He wore golden boots, golden trousers, and a golden jacket. His hair was blond and styled in a quiff, and his skin was so fair it was almost luminous.

Kasper staggered back in amazement and fell against the bell.

"Well—hey there!—thank you, moonlit dude," the King said, taking the pie from Kasper. "No black eyes tonight."

Kasper blinked and rubbed his eyes. The gold had dazzled him so much that it made his eyes water. As his vision cleared, he studied the King closer.

Kasper guessed the King to be about thirteen years old. He looked very strong under all those shimmering clothes. His eyes were frosty blue, like fragments of summer sky.

"Well—hey there!—I want to tell you something," the King said, licking cream from his lips. "The whole world is divided into the yucks and the yums." He swallowed some more pie. "Did you know that, moonlit dude?" The King took a step towards Kasper and stared down at him.

Kasper looked up at the King. "N-n-no," he managed.

"Well, it just happens to be true," he said. A piece of banana started to slide down his chin. "The yum things include people telling me I'm their best friend and people cooking me yummy Banoffi pie." The banana slice was now hanging from the King's chin by a thread of honey. "The yuck things include people telling me I'm not their best friend and people cooking me yucky Banoffi pie."

The piece of banana was swinging like a pendulum from the King's chin by now. Kasper couldn't take his eyes off it. He wanted to tell the King but didn't know how.

The King scooped the last handful of pie into his mouth and licked the plate. The dangling banana fell from King Streetwise's chin and landed on Kasper's forehead. Kasper was too nervous to remove it.

When the King had licked the plate clean, he threw it to one side and smiled at Kasper. "Well—hey there!—where did you learn to make a pie like that, moonlit dude?" he asked.

"At home," replied Kasper.

"Home?" roared the King. "Don't say home! It's the yuckiest thing of all." He glared down at Kasper. "Say, 'I have no home.' Go on!" His voice was a gentle purr now. "Well—hey there!—say it for me."

Kasper stared at the gold sequins. "I . . . I . . ." he stammered.

"You don't need a home," said King Streetwise. "Not with me around. I'm all you need. I offer you The Gloom. Don't you want that?"

"I . . . I . . ."

"Well—hey there!—in the Gloom you can eat what you want, wear what you want, and say what you want. Don't you want that?"

"I . . . I . . ."

"In the Gloom there're a million lights and a million smells and a million people to play with. Well—hey there!—be honest with yourself! Say you want it."

The gold sequins seemed to be getting brighter.

"I . . . I . . ."

"And—hey there!—there's me! Don't try to make out you don't want to be near my golden light?"

"Y . . . yes!" said Kasper. "I do!"

"Then say it! Say 'I have no home.' "

"I . . . I . . ."

"SAY IT!"

And, suddenly, Kasper wanted to say it. He wanted to

please King Streetwise. He would have said anything to make him happy.

"I have no home," Kasper said finally.

It was such a relief to say it.

"Well—hey there!—yum to my ears," said the King, smiling. "By the way, you've got a bit of banana on your forehead." He licked it off. "Yum, yum, yum."

Kasper was feeling more relaxed now. Somehow, saying he had no home had calmed him down.

The King sat by one of the openings and stared at the lights of the City beyond. He touched his chest and let out a painful "Ouch."

"What is it?" asked Kasper. He was afraid the pie had given the King indigestion.

King Streetwise glanced at Kasper. "Why don't you just tell me your name, little moonlit dude?" he asked.

"Kasper," Kasper told him.

"Well—hey there!—come here, Kasper."

Kasper went to the King's side.

"I have a heartache, Kasper," said the King. "A very painful heartache—ouch!"

"What is it?" inquired Kasper.

"Look out there," said the King, indicating the City. "Out there are the Lost. Lost little moonlit dudes. Just like yourself. And— hey there!—I care for them, Kasper. You believe that, don't you?"

"Certainly," Kasper said.

The King put his arm around Kasper's shoulders. "All I want to do is be their friend. But there are some moonlit dudes who don't want my friendship."

"Impossible!" exclaimed Kasper.

"Well—hey there!—very possible, I'm afraid, moonlit dude," the King sighed, hugging him. "And it gives me a— ouch!" he said, clutching his chest. "It gives me a terrible heartache to think that, somewhere, some moonlit dude doesn't like me."

"I like you!" cried Kasper.

The King held him tighter. The sequins on his jacket scraped against Kasper's cheek.

"And am I your best friend in the universe?" asked the King.

"Absolutely!"

"Say it."

"You're my best friend in the universe."

"Well—hey there!—you can be my cook," the King said. "Would you like that?"

"Certainly," said Kasper.

"Knew you would!" The King released his grip on Kasper. "That's what I do, you see. I give the Lost jobs to do. That's what we all need. Jobs. Don't you think so?"

"Certainly," Kasper agreed.

The King walked over to the bell and leaned against it. His sky blue eyes looked very sad.

"What's wrong?" asked Kasper.

"Well—hey there!—my friend," said the King softly. "I'm thinking of the biggest heartache I have. A heartache so big that, in comparison, icebergs are snowflakes, mountains are pebbles, and stars in the sky mere sparks." He embraced the bell as if it was a living thing. "Ouch!" he cried. "Well—hey there!—ouch!"

His voice was so passionate it almost made the bell ring.

"Would it help if you told me about it?" inquired Kasper.

"Oh, you don't want to know," the King sighed. "I'm here to care for everyone else, but—hey there!—no one cares for me."

"I care," Kasper told him.

The King smiled. "Then I'll tell you," he said. "I'll tell you why I am the saddest and most lonely moonlit dude in the whole moonlit universe."

The King positioned himself until the shaft of moonlight lit him like a spotlight.

"Well—hey there!—once," said the King, sighing, "I loved a moonlit creature. And her name was . . . well—hey there!—Hushabye Brightwing."

*H*ushabye Brightwing," echoed Kasper. It was the most beautiful name he'd ever heard.

So beautiful, in fact, that Kasper had to say it again. Slower, this time, relishing the sound like it was something sweet to taste. "Hush-a-bye Bright-wing." He tingled all over.

"Well—hey there!—Hushabye had the prettiest hair in the Gloom," continued the King. "The prettiest, longest, reddest hair you've ever seen. Every morning I would stroke it and say, 'Good morning, my love.' And every night, I'd stroke it and say, 'Good night, my love.' "

The King clutched at his chest. "Oh, the heartache, the heartache," he said. "She was going to be my Queen, you see. What a perfect couple we'd have made. King Streetwise and Queen Hushabye. Rulers of the Gloom together." The King looked down, his eyes full of tears. "But then he stole her."

"Who stole her?" asked Kasper.

"One of my Argonauts."

"The fifth Argonaut!" cried Kasper. "That's why there's five of everything."

"Five of everything?"

"Downstairs," Kasper explained. "There's five mattresses and five plates and five—"

"Well—hey there!—I ordered those things to be burnt!" King Streetwise roared. "If those things aren't burnt at once, there'll be black eyes by morning. I don't want anything in the Palace to remind me of that treacherous, yucky Argonaut," he said. "He kidnapped the thing I loved. He turned her against me—ouch! He poisoned her mind—ouch! Now there's no beautiful red hair to stroke at night and in the morning. Now—oh, ouch! Ouch! Ouch—I'm all alone!"

"You're not alone!" cried Kasper. "You've got me!"

"Well—hey there!—that's right," said the King, smiling. "And I'll have you forever, won't I?"

"Certainly! How can anyone want to leave a friend like you?"

"The yucky Argonaut did."

"Then he was stupid."

"Well—hey there!—that's the truth. All he was interested in was his quiff. I can hear his voice now. 'Don't touch my perfect quiff, man.' That's all he would say. . . ."

"Heartthrob!" Kasper gasped.

"Who told you that?" snapped the King. "I've forbidden his yucky name ever to be mentioned in the Palace. Did one of the Argonauts or Jingo tell you? If they did, there'll be black eyes by morning—"

"They didn't say a word."

"Then how . . . ?"

"I know him!" Kasper said. "At least . . . well, I've *met* him. You see, he stole things from me as well."

"What things?" asked the King.

"Well, first he stole my roses—"

"Roses!" cried King Streetwise. "They're for her. For my Hushabye Brightwing! She loves roses! There used to be roses all around the Palace. It was her garden. Now I can't even smell or see a rose without it breaking my heart. Well—hey there!—Kasper," he continued, falling to his knees, "this heartache is too much for my glorious and golden body to bear."

"But I know where to find Heartthrob!" cried Kasper. "It's a place Heartthrob calls the Arch."

The King stared at Kasper. "What's this . . . Arch?" he asked.

"It's a bridge! A railway bridge! Heartthrob lives behind a poster of a tropical island! That's where you'll find him and . . . your Hushabye."

The King jumped to his feet.

"Yum!" he cried at the top of his voice. "Yum, yum!"

The King picked up Kasper and started rushing down the stairs.

"Well—hey there!—what a wonderful friend you are!" cried the King. "Not only do you cook me the best Banoffi pie in all the Gloom, but you also tell me where to find my love."

They reached the bottom of the stairs.

The King rushed up to his Throne and sat in it.

He put Kasper down beside him.

"Tonight," said the King, smiling, "we're going to hunt for my love! And you're going to join us. We're going to find my love and teach that treacherous, yucky Heart-throb a lesson. Shall we do that?"

"Absolutely!" cried Kasper eagerly.

The King embraced Kasper. "My friend!" he said. Then he screamed, "ARGONAUTS!"

His voice echoed around the Palace.

"ARGONAUTS . . . GONAUTS . . . ONAUTS . . . NAUTS . . . AUTS . . . SSSSS."

he next second Jingo appeared.

Closely followed by Skinnybones.

Then Poodlecut.

Then Fingerpoppin.

And, finally, Knucklehead. They were all huddled together, trembling with fear as they approached the Throne.

The King chuckled. "Well—hey there!—look at those poor moonlit dudes." He glanced at Kasper and whispered, "They think your pie was yucky and I'm going to give them black eyes."

Jingo and the Argonauts came to a halt in front of the Throne.

"The pie was yum," the King assured them. "No black eyes tonight."

The Argonauts sighed with relief.

"Well done, squire."

"Good show, old bean."

"Bravo, chief."

"Woof, matey."

Then, "Congratulations, Master Kasper," said Jingo.

The King's smile grew wider. "But even yummier than the pie," he said, "is the news that Kasper has given me." Still wider the smile. "He's told me where to find something. Well—hey there!—can you guess what that something is?"

The Argonauts thought for a while, talking softly amongst themselves, then shook their heads.

"No, squire."

"No, old bean."

"No, chief."

"Woof, matey."

Then, "Afraid not, King," said Jingo.

"HUSHABYE!" cried King Streetwise, jumping to his feet. "He told me where to find the love of my life!" Then he glared at the Argonauts. "And I've told you before not to call me squire or old bean or chief or matey. I am the King and that's what you call me! King!"

"Sorry, squi—I mean, King."

"Sorry, old bea—I mean, King."

"Sorry, chie—I mean, King."

"Woof, mat—I mean, King."

And then they started chattering excitedly, their voices overlapping into one frantic rush of sound.

The only two words Kasper could make out were *Hushabye* and *Heartthrob*. The whispered names echoed round the Palace like living things.

"FETCH ME THE MAP!" boomed the King to Jingo.

Jingo went to a nearby cupboard and returned with a sheet of rolled paper. He got to his knees and spread it out in front of the Throne.

It was a map of the City: those areas known as the

Glitter were colored yellow, and those areas known as the Gloom were colored blue.

The King stared down at it. "A bridge," he said thoughtfully, running his fingers through his blond quiff. He glanced at Kasper. "A railway bridge on the edge of the Scream, you say?"

"Absolutely, King," replied Kasper.

The King continued staring at the map. "Well—hey there!—there are only three," he said. "Three railway bridges on the edge of the Scream in the whole of the Gloom." He jumped over the map and started running down the aisle. He spun around and around as he ran, whirling between the candles and broken wooden pews like a golden tornado. "Tonight we will go to the first of the three bridges!" he cried. "If my Hushabye isn't there, we'll go to the second bridge tomorrow. And then the third

bridge the night after that." Still spinning and spinning. "Well—hey there!—within three nights I'll see the prettiest hair in the Gloom again!"

The King knocked one of the candles over.

It fell into a pile of wood.

Instantly there was smoke, and the wood began to smoulder.

"Gracious me!" exclaimed Jingo, rushing to stamp out the flame.

He'd just finished doing so when the King knocked over another candle.

Again it fell into a pile of wood.

Again smoke.

"Gracious me!"

Still King Streetwise breezed around the Palace crying, "Hushabye! Hushabye! Your Palace awaits you!"

"If you'll permit me," Jingo said anxiously. "There won't be any Palace left if you keep knocking the candles over—oh, gracious me!"

Another candle fell.

More sparks.

More smoke.

Kasper rushed to help Jingo stamp it out.

Suddenly, the King stopped spinning and cried, "Get my cloak, Jingo!"

"A pleasure," said Jingo. He went to a cupboard in the corner of the Palace.

When Jingo returned, he was holding a magnificent cloak covered with golden sequins. He draped it around the King's shoulders.

The King ran his hands over the golden sequins. "Yum!" he said softly, his eyes half-closed. Then, slowly, King Streetwise strode over to Kasper and stared down at him. "You are my best friend," he said, patting Kasper's head. He carefully plucked a golden sequin from his cloak. "Well—hey there!—this is yours."

Kasper held out his hand.

The King pressed the sequin into Kasper's palm.

Kasper stared at the tiny spot of gold, then up at the King. The King appeared twice as tall in his glorious cloak. Kasper wanted to say thank you but was too overwhelmed.

The Argonauts stopped whispering amongst themselves and stared, their mouths open.

King Streetwise spun round and cried, "Prepare the Chariot!"

Instantly the Palace echoed with scampering footsteps.

Jingo rushed over to Kasper and said, "This way." He led Kasper to the back of the Palace. "The King has never given anyone a sequin before," he said. "You must be very honored."

"Absolutely," Kasper assured him.

Jingo opened a door. "After you," he said, bowing slightly.

"Certainly not," Kasper insisted. "After you."

"Gracious me, no! I can't possibly go before someone with a sequin." And Jingo bowed even lower, waiting for Kasper to walk through the door.

"Well, in that case . . . thank you," said Kasper a little uneasily, and walked outside.

A thick tangle of roseless bushes was facing him. Only this time a small area had been cleared.

In the middle of this clearing was the Chariot.

The Chariot had a wooden base with two large car tires on either side; its main body was constructed of tin cans. The cans had been painted gold, and glinted in the moonlight.

Knucklehead pushed past Kasper. He had the two dogs, Moonglow and Stardust, with him. Carefully (and muttering "woof-woof" constantly), he harnessed the animals to the front of the Chariot.

Then the King strode by Kasper and jumped up onto the Chariot. He was holding a whip that he swished through the air. (Actually, it was a stick with a bit of string tied to one end. But, from a distance, it looked like a real whip.)

The King flicked the whip, and the dogs started pulling the Chariot forwards.

"TO HUSHABYE!" cried King Streetwise.

They were going down a long street.

On either side were houses, deserted and crumbling. Through holes in the walls Kasper could see smashed televisions, cracked plates, and shattered mirrors.

The King flicked the whip.

Moonglow and Stardust pulled the Chariot even faster.

It turned a corner and went down another street.

Again, it was deserted and full of ruined houses.

The Argonauts were all running behind the Chariot, trying to get in front of each other.

"Out of my way, squire."

"You're in my way, old bean."

"You're holding me back, chief."

"Woof, matey!"

Jingo was getting breathless now. He was smaller than the others and found it difficult to keep up. Also, his jacket tails kept tripping him.

"Forgive me," spluttered Jingo, stumbling against Kasper. "I know I'm not even worthy of touching someone with a sequin. . . . It's just that . . ." He stumbled once more and nearly fell over. "Gracious me!" he exclaimed. "I'm . . . finding it . . . hard . . . to . . . keep . . . up!"

"I'll carry you," Kasper told him. "Jump on my back."

"Oh, no!" exclaimed Jingo, gasping for breath. "I can't . . . possibly . . . allow . . . someone with a sequin to—"

"Forget the sequin!" snapped Kasper.

"Well . . . if you insist," gasped Jingo. He clambered on Kasper's back. "A million thanks."

The Chariot turned a corner.

Another deserted street.

More disintegrating houses.

"We have to keep to the empty streets," Jingo whispered

in Kasper's ear. "This is our world. The world of the Lost."

"But . . . so much of it is broken," Kasper noticed.

"Very true," Jingo agreed. "But sometimes broken things are the most beautiful."

King Streetwise flicked the whip again.

The Chariot moved faster.

It turned a corner.

Another deserted street.

Kasper could hear the dogs growling.

Then . . .

"STOP!" cried the King.

The Chariot came to a halt.

The King pointed.

At the end of the street was a bridge. A train thundered across it, then disappeared into the distance.

"The first bridge!" cried King Streetwise.

Kasper stepped forward to get a better look. He couldn't tell if it was the right bridge or not.

Yes, it was a railway bridge. And, yes (from the sound of the traffic), it was near the Scream. But, at the moment, that's all he could tell.

The King flicked his whip (gently this time), and, slowly, the Chariot moved forward.

Stardust and Moonglow were panting very hard, saliva dribbling from their fangs.

Knucklehead walked beside them. "Woof—woof," he said, stroking them.

Kasper's heart was beating very fast.

As they got closer, Kasper could see people under the bridge. There were about seven of them. All wrapped in newspapers and asleep in cardboard boxes.

There was a yellow street lamp nearby. But it was faulty. It flickered on and off. When it went off, the only light came from the moon. Which was blue. And, when it flashed on, everything became yellow again. Blue. Yellow. Blue. Yellow.

It made Kasper giddy just looking at it.

They were almost under the bridge now.

Kasper could see that the homeless were all about his age.

Another train thundered by.

It made Kasper's ears ring.

But the sleeping Lost did not wake.

They must be used to it, thought Kasper.

Yellow. Blue. Yellow. Blue.

"WAKE UP!"
boomed the King.
His voice reverberated
under the bridge.

The Lost opened
their eyes and
struggled out of
their cardboard
boxes.

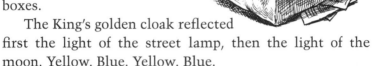

The King's golden cloak reflected first the light of the street lamp, then the light of the moon. Yellow. Blue. Yellow. Blue.

"Well—hey there!—listen to me, you sleepy Lost," announced the King. "I am here to find the love of my life. Hushabye Brightwing!"

The Argonauts shuffled forward.

"Hushabye, squires."

"With the beautiful hair, old beans."

"Love of his life, chiefs."

"Woof, mateys."

Kasper could see that the Argonauts' faces were twitching with excitement: eyes wide, nostrils flared, tongues licking lips.

"Far be it from me," began Jingo, whispering in Kasper's ear, "to tell someone with a sequin what to do, but you can put me down now if you want to."

Kasper did so, then looked at the walls under the bridge. There were several posters. But none of a tropical island.

Good heavens! thought Kasper. This is not the Arch.

"Do you know where my Hushabye is?" the King was demanding.

The newly awakened Lost shook their heads.

The King jumped from his Chariot and approached them.

Kasper said, "This isn't the right bridge."

The King glared at him. His eyes changed color with the light. Yellow. Blue. Yellow. Blue.

"There's no poster of a tropical island," explained Kasper. "So Hushabye isn't here!"

The Argonauts muttered amongst themselves.

"Wrong bridge, squires."

"Wrong bridge, old beans."

"Wrong bridge, chiefs."

"Woof, mateys."

Then, "Gracious me!" muttered Jingo.

The King collapsed to his knees and clutched at his chest.

"Ouch!" he whined. "Another night without my Hushabye! Another night before I see her pretty hair—ouch, ouch, ouch!"

Then he glared at the Lost. "Tell me, you sleepy and trembling moonlit dudes, do you know who I am?"

The Lost were too afraid to speak.

"Well—hey there!—I'm your King!" yelled Streetwise. "And that means you belong to me! That means . . . I'm your best friend!" He pointed at the Lost. "Say it!" he demanded. "Soothe the ouch in my chest. Turn my totally yucky night into a little bit of a yum! Say 'King Streetwise is my best friend!' "

Stardust and Moonglow snarled.

"Say it!"

Still the Lost said nothing.

The King got to his feet and raised his fist in the air. His rings gleamed. Yellow. Blue. Yellow. Blue. His eyes were raging.

The Argonauts muttered. . . .

"They're not going to say it, squires."

"Nothing, old beans."

"Not a word, chiefs."

"Woof, mateys."

Then, "Gracious me!" said Jingo. "Silence!"

The dogs snarled louder.

The King raised his fist in the air. "TEAR THEIR CARDBOARD," he screeched. "TEAR IT ALL!"

And, suddenly, the tunnel was a cauldron of noise and panic.

The Argonauts rushed forward and started ripping the cardboard boxes the Lost had been sleeping in.

The Lost screamed.

The dogs howled.

The Argonauts laughed.

The street lamp flickered.

Blue. Yellow. Blue. Yellow.

"Please, don't," begged Kasper, tugging at the King's cloak. "You can't force people to be your friend."

But King Streetwise wasn't listening. "I WILL TEAR ALL THE CARDBOARD IN THE GLOOM UNTIL EVERYONE SAYS I'M THEIR BEST FRIEND," he roared. "TEAR IT! TEAR IT! TEAR IT!"

Kasper rushed up to Skinnybones and pleaded, "Don't do it."

"It's what King Streetwise wants, squire," said Skinnybones. "I'll do anything he says. Won't you?"

"I . . . I thought I would," replied Kasper. "But . . . not this! This isn't the way to make friends. Stop! Stop!"

"Part of my job, squire."

"Mine too, old bean."

"Mine too, chief."

"Woof, matey."

And they continued tearing and tearing.

Jingo tugged at Kasper's sleeve. "If you'll permit me," he said, talking loudly to overcome the screaming and shouting, "it's best to let them get on with it."

"But it's terrible!" cried Kasper.

"Far be it from me to argue with someone with a sequin," Jingo said, bowing slightly, "but this is the King's way."

A train thundered by overhead.

The tunnel was a nightmare of noise and light now.

Screaming!

Yellow!

Howling!

Blue!

Suddenly, Kasper could bear it no longer.

He ran!

He didn't know where he was going.

He just ran and ran as fast as he could.

I've got to get away, he thought. King Streetwise is not a friend.

Vroom!

Kasper looked all round him.

He'd run straight onto the Scream!
Cars and lorries whizzed past him.
Vrooom! went their engines.
Beep! went their horns.
Kasper leaped out of the way.
Everything was spinning around him.
Vroooom!

Beeep!

Car headlights blinded him. Tires screeched. He ran and ran. His mind yelled, "Help me! Help me!"

Vroom!

Beep!

Screech!

Kasper tripped up a curb. He stumbled forward, half walking, half falling.

Finally, he crashed to the ground.

He lay there for a while, the cold pavement against his cheek.

When he'd got his breath back, he sat up and checked himself for cuts and bruises. Just a tiny graze on the palm of one hand. He unclenched his other hand.

The golden sequin was still there. He tried to pluck it off, but it seemed to be stuck to his skin.

I don't want anything to do with King Streetwise, he thought. Go away, sequin! Go!

Eventually, he freed the sequin.

And a gentle breeze lifted it into the air.

It floated away. And landed on . . .

A boot.

A pointed black boot of someone standing in the shadows.

Kasper got to his feet and looked closer.

I'm under a bridge, he thought. A railway bridge! And there— Yes! There's a poster of a tropical island. . . . It's the Arch!

Kasper stared at the figure in the shadows.

It picked the sequin from the boot, then stepped out of the shadows.

"What do you think of my suntan, man?" asked Heart-throb.

Kasper was so relieved to see Heartthrob that he rushed over to hug him. "Oh, Heartthrob," he cried. "Heartthrob!"

"Careful, man," warned Heartthrob, backing away. "You'll make me drop my melon."

It was only then Kasper noticed the large green melon under Heartthrob's arm.

"Found it in a dustbin," Heartthrob explained. "Just needs a bit of a clean." He looked at the dirt on Kasper's suit. "Talking about a bit of a clean," he commented, "you're a wreck, man."

"And it's all because of you!" snapped Kasper. (Now that he'd gotten over his surprise, he remembered why he'd come to the Gloom in the first place.) "I came here to find you. But, instead, I found—"

"King Streetwise!" interrupted Heartthrob, lifting his finger in the air. The golden sequin was on the end. "Am I right or am I right?"

Kasper sighed. "I don't know what's right anymore," he said. "First I thought you were my friend, then I changed my mind. Then I thought the King was my friend, but then I changed my mind about him as well. And now . . . now I'm not sure about anything. I never knew that making friends would be this confusing."

A gust of wind blew the sequin from Heartthrob's finger. It shot into the darkness like a glittering insect.

"The King said you stole Hushabye Brightwing from him," Kasper said. "Is that true?"

Heartthrob went to the poster of the tropical island and lifted it. There was a small hole in the wall behind. "Follow me, man," he said. "You can ask her yourself." And he disappeared through the hole.

Ask Hushabye! thought Kasper. That means actually *see* the prettiest hair in the Gloom!

And as quickly as he could, he scampered after Heart-throb.

He found himself in a stone chamber illuminated by candles. There was a large round mirror (with many cracks) propped against the far wall and a cardboard box in the middle. The box was very big and had a door and windows cut into it. All around the box were—

"My roses!" Kasper gasped.

Most of the roses were brown and withered. But some (probably the ones Kasper had given Heartthrob the night before) were still in full bloom.

Heartthrob put the melon down and knocked on the cardboard box. "The boy from the Nothing's here to see you, man!" he said.

"Righto, Brother Heartthrob," said a girl's voice from inside the box.

And the next second, she scampered out.

She was about twelve years old and wearing a simple black dress and the biggest boots Kasper had ever seen. So big, in fact, they laced all the way up to her knees. But the most surprising thing about the girl was her hair.

Or, rather, the lack of it.

Because she was totally bald!

"He came here to find me, man," said Heartthrob, going over to the cracked mirror. "But Streetwise got to him first." He looked at his reflection. "Lovely-jubbly." Then added, "And Streetwise told him I stole you from him."

"Silly, silly!" She glanced at Kasper. "Streetwise probably told you I loved him as well," she said. "Right?"

Kasper nodded.

"Silly, silly, silly!" snapped the girl. "Well, there's a lot of explaining to do. But first things first. I'm Sister Hushabye. And you are Brother . . . ?"

"Kasper," said Kasper. "But I'm not your brother."

"I call everyone my brother or sister," Hushabye explained. "All the Lost should be one big family. That's what I believe anyway. Now then, Brother Kasper, you must be hungry. Do you like melon?"

"I'm not sure," Kasper replied, still looking at her bald head. "I eat yellow food mainly."

Hushabye stared at him in amazement. "What a lot of silliness!" she exclaimed. "Brother Heartthrob told me what your life was like with your mother, but it all sounded such nonsense I thought he was joking." She picked up the melon, then hurled it to the ground. It broke into many pieces. Inside was red and juicy. "Now, eat this," she said, handing him a piece.

Kasper took a bite.

"Like it, Brother Kasper?" asked Hushabye.

"Very much," Kasper replied, juice trickling down his chin.

"There you are! Only yellow food indeed! The world is full of such silliness sometimes. Talking of silliness, come and eat, Brother Heartthrob. You must be bored of your reflection by now."

"Never!" cried Heartthrob, touching his quiff. "With all these cracks in the mirror, I can see a hundred Heartthrobs. And every one of them is interesting."

"You're about as interesting as a sugar cube," Hushabye told him, sitting on the floor. "He's always been vain," she said to Kasper, "but since you gave him that suntan, he's been unbearable."

Kasper sat beside her and started eating another piece of melon.

"Now then, Brother Kasper," began Hushabye, picking up a piece of melon for herself, "what other lies has that silly Streetwise told you?"

"Well . . ." began Kasper, chewing, "he said you had pretty hair—"

"Don't say that word!"

"What word?"

"*Pretty!*" she told him. "That's all Brother Streetwise said to me when I had hair. 'Oh, you've got the prettiest hair in the Gloom.' Uggh." She shuddered all over as if she'd just swallowed a mouthful of vinegar. "Who wants to be pretty?" she demanded. "Anyway, I've shaved all my hair off now, and I hope I never hear another *pretty* for as long as I live."

Kasper paused for a second, then asked, "So . . . what really happened? Between you and Streetwise and Heartthrob. Please tell me."

"Very well," said Hushabye. "And, believe me, I'm the only one you'll get any sense out of in this place."

"I talk sense!" interrupted Heartthrob.

"Be quiet, Brother Heartthrob," said Hushabye. "I've got socks that talk more sense than you. Besides, I've got a story to tell. . . ."

Hushabye took a deep breath, then began. "When I first arrived in the Gloom, I was all alone—"

"Were you scared?" asked Kasper.

"A little bit, yes, Brother Kasper. But I didn't get flustered. I just walked the streets looking for somewhere to sleep. I tried one old house, but it was full of rats. Not a sensible place at all. Then I saw an old building at the end of a dark street. There was a spire on top of the building, and it was surrounded by roses—"

"The Palace!" cried Kasper excitedly.

"Correct, Brother Kasper. Although it wasn't called the Palace then. This was before Streetwise appeared on the scene."

"So did you live in the Palace alone?"

"I did, Brother Kasper. And very happy I was, too. I got the big oven downstairs working—so I could cook. I found a cupboard of candles—so I had light. And I mended the plumbing—so I could wash. But you know what I liked most about the place, Brother Kasper?"

"What?" asked Kasper.

"The roses! I would prune them and water them every day. And, at night, I could smell them. I felt safe and happy surrounded by my roses. But, one day, my happiness went kaput!"

"What happened?"

"There was a knock at the door. I opened it and saw a boy standing outside. He had blond hair—"

"Streetwise!" Kasper gasped.

"Correct, Brother Kasper. But not Streetwise as you know him now. When I first saw him, he was shivering and hungry and very dirty. He said he'd run away from home and hadn't eaten for three days. He'd seen me getting some food from a dustbin and followed me back.

He asked if he could come in. And I . . . I felt sorry for him."

"So you let him in," said Kasper.

"The silliest thing I've ever done." Hushabye sighed. "Some more melon, Brother Kasper?"

"Thank you," said Kasper, taking an extra-large chunk. "So you and Streetwise lived alone in the Palace for a while?"

"Correct, Brother Kasper," she said. "I taught him how to survive in the Gloom." She picked a melon pip from her teeth. "And then he started stroking my hair— Oh, it makes me shiver just to think of it. And then, one night, he told me he loved me. His nonsense knew no bounds."

"What did you do?" asked Kasper, munching melon.

"I laughed," replied Hushabye.

"I bet Streetwise was angry."

"Correct, Brother Kasper. He jumped up and down and screamed at me, 'If you don't love me, you can't be my Queen.'

" 'Queen of what?' I asked him.

" 'Queen of the Gloom!' he replied.

" 'And who says you're the King?' I asked him.

" 'I say!' shrieked Streetwise. 'I always knew I was destined to be King of the Gloom. That's why I'm here. To rule the Lost.' "

"What did you do then?" asked Kasper.

"I laughed again," replied Hushabye. "I couldn't help myself. I'd never heard such silliness in all my born days. King of the Gloom, indeed! Ruler of the Lost! What nonsense! But, that night, Streetwise rushed out of the building, and when he returned later, he had another boy with him. He was short and muttering 'Gracious me!' over and over—"

"Jingo!" cried Kasper.

"Correct, Brother Kasper. Streetwise had gone out to the Gloom, found Jingo, and brought him back to be his . . . well, his butler he said, but I call it his slave. The next night Streetwise came back with another boy. This one was tall and thin and called everyone squire—"

"Skinnybones!" cried Kasper.

"Correct, Brother Kasper. The next night Streetwise came back with another boy. He had long, curly black hair and huge handlelike ears. He called everyone old bean—"

"Poodlecut!" cried Kasper.

"Correct, Brother Kasper. The next night Streetwise returned with another boy. His fingers went *pop*—"

"Fingerpoppin!"

"Correct, Brother Kasper. The next night, yet another boy. He had two dogs with him and only said 'woof'—"

"Knucklehead!"

"Correct, Brother Kasper. And, all the time, Streetwise was becoming more and more convinced he was the King of the Gloom. And why shouldn't he? With all those boys following him around and waiting on him hand and foot."

"But still you wouldn't say you loved him?" asked Kasper.

"Of course not, Brother Kasper. I could never lie about something like that."

"So . . . why didn't you leave?"

"I was going to, Brother Kasper. But then, one night, he came home with a new boy. A boy with a perfect quiff—"

"Heartthrob!" cried Kasper.

"Spot on, man." Heartthrob came over and sat beside them. He picked up a piece of melon and bit into it. "Streetwise brought me back to the Palace to be one of his Argonauts."

"Argonauts!" cried Hushabye. "Those poor boys!" She looked at Kasper. "You know what the Argonauts are, don't you, Brother Kasper?"

"Jingo said they were Streetwise's soldiers."

"Oh, they're more than that. Argonauts are the children Streetwise has *tempted* to run away from home!"

"What!" Kasper gasped, nearly choking on some melon.

"It's true, Brother Kasper. Streetwise wants to be King of the Gloom and rule all the Lost. But what gives him the biggest thrill is *tempting* children to run away. That's when he feels the most powerful."

"And he calls them Argonauts?"

"Correct, Brother Kasper. That's why Jingo can never be an Argonaut. He had no real home to be tempted away from. He was already in the Gloom. But the others— Skinnybones, Poodlecut, Fingerpoppin, Knucklehead—"

"And Heartthrob!" said Kasper.

"Correct. They were all *tempted* to run away." Hushabye took a deep breath. "By now, I realized how totally silly Streetwise was. So I stayed to try to stop him. And I felt the only Argonaut who might help me was Brother Heartthrob. He was the one who looked the least happy. But it was too late. There was no stopping Streetwise. He was wearing those silly golden clothes. And talking in that totally silly way. 'Well—hey there!—what yucks and yums there are in the world, my moonlit dudes,' " she said, mimicking Streetwise's voice.

Kasper laughed.

"You're right to laugh, Brother Kasper," she said. "It *is* totally silly! Nobody talks like that! Moonlit dudes indeed. I laughed when I heard it, too. I laughed when he kept asking me to tell him I loved him. As if I could love such a silly thing as him. And then . . . then, one night, he did the silliest thing of all."

"What?" asked Kasper.

"He and the Argonauts caught hold of me and carried me up to the spire. And they . . . oh, the silly, silly, silliness of it! . . . they put me under the bell. He kept me prisoner," she said, "trapped under the bell in the spire."

"I saw that bell!" cried Kasper, accidentally spitting a melon pip at Hushabye. "It looked very heavy."

"It was, Brother Kasper," Hushabye said, wiping the pip from her cheek. "Too heavy for me to lift alone. So I was stuck under it, with my head sticking out the hole at the top. King Streetwise said he was going to keep me trapped there until I said I loved him and agreed to be his Queen."

"But you didn't say it?" asked Kasper.

"Never!" replied Hushabye.

"And so . . . Heartthrob helped you escape?"

"Not at first," said Hushabye. "All he did was come up to the spire every hour to look at his reflection in the shiny surface of the bell. Day after day I tried to convince him to escape with me. But he wouldn't. He was too scared."

"Scared! Me? Don't make me laugh," insisted Heartthrob, melon juice dribbling down his chin. "I'm a courageous Heartthrob!"

"I've seen cream cakes more courageous than you!" snapped Hushabye. "It was the golden helmets that made you help me, nothing else!"

"How?" asked Kasper.

"Because Streetwise wanted him to wear one like all the other Argonauts," Hushabye explained. "And, of course, he wouldn't. Because it would spoil—"

"His perfect quiff!" cried Kasper.

"I couldn't wear that helmet, man," Heartthrob said. "It made me look stupid."

"You look stupid anyway," Hushabye told him.

"No I don't, man. I'm a tasty Heartthrob."

"You're about as tasty as a worm sandwich," said Hushabye, picking up another piece of melon. "And a scaredy-cat worm sandwich at that!"

"But Heartthrob helped you escape eventually," said Kasper.

Hushabye nodded. "Eventually, yes. One night Brother Heartthrob helped me lift the bell, and we ran away," she said. Then added, "Although, as I said, I'm sure he was more interested in saving his quiff."

"I did it for you as well!" Heartthrob insisted. His

mouth was so full of melon, he could barely speak. "And look at all the other things I've done for you!"

"Like what?" asked Hushabye, raising an eyebrow.

"Well . . . I . . . I found this place to hide."

"No, Brother Heartthrob," Hushabye told him. "*I* found this hiding place. You were too busy touching your quiff at the time."

"Well . . . what about . . ." Heartthrob thought for a while. Then he cried, "The roses! I got you the roses so you'd feel at home."

Hushabye smiled and nodded. "That's correct," she said. "You did get me the roses. But what I *really* want is a *plan*."

"A plan?" asked Kasper.

"Yes, Brother Kasper. A sensible plan so we can put an end to Streetwise and all his silliness. I'm fed up with hiding from him here."

"But we have to!" interrupted Heartthrob excitedly. "It's too dangerous out there. There's only two of us. And Streetwise has got the Argonauts and Jingo and—"

"All right, all right, Brother Heartthrob," cut in Hushabye, trying to calm him down. "Don't panic!"

"Panic? Me? Don't make me laugh."

"But you are! Every time I mention a plan, you go all pale. You're so pale now, even your suntan has gone!"

"It has?" Heartthrob rushed to the mirror to check.

"Only teasing!" giggled Hushabye.

Heartthrob came back and spat a melon pip at her.

Hushabye chuckled and spat a pip back.

Then Kasper started giggling and spat a pip at Heartthrob as well.

And soon they were all laughing and squealing and spitting pips at each other.

"Mind my quiff, man!" complained Heartthrob.

Which made them spit pips at him all the more.

They spat pips until there were no more pips left to spit.

Afterwards, they sat on the ground, leaning against each other, getting their breath back.

"That was fun!" Kasper gasped.

Suddenly, everything started to shake.

It was like an earthquake.

Kasper jumped to his feet in alarm and stared at Hushabye and Heartthrob.

But they didn't seem worried at all.

They just glanced up . . . up to where the railway was.

"The first train of the morning," Hushabye said, getting to her feet.

"Morning!" exclaimed Kasper.

And he rushed over to the hole in the wall and peeped outside.

Sure enough, the sun had risen.

"I should go home," Kasper said.

"I'd like you to stay here," said Hushabye softly.

"Me too, man," Heartthrob agreed.

"But Pumpkin won't know what to do without me and . . ." Kasper's voice trailed away for a second. Then he continued. "It's been a wonderful night. Odd, but wonderful. And I want to see you again! Please visit me tomorrow. Both of you. I'll cook you something. You'll be safe out in the Nothing. King Streetwise will never find you there. Please say you'll come."

"Sure, man," said Heartthrob. "I can improve my suntan."

"I'll come as well, Brother Kasper," said Hushabye, smiling.

And, with that, Kasper crawled through the hole.

He walked out from under the bridge and—looking very carefully—crossed the Scream, into the Nothing.

The trail of rose petals was still there from the night before, although they were turning brown now and glistening with morning dew.

Kasper was so tired by the time he got home, he barely had enough energy to open the garden gate.

As he climbed the stairs to his bedroom, he heard Pumpkin call "A facial!" He peeked into her room. She was fast asleep.

"I'm home, Pumpkin," he whispered.

21

Kasper dreamed of golden sequins and tin cans.

"Honey!"

—and howling dogs and broken bells—

"Wake up, honey!"

—and candles and chariots—

"WAKE UP, HONEY!"

Kasper's eyes clicked open.

Pumpkin was standing beside his bed, shaking him.

"Pumpkin!" he cried, rubbing his eyes. "Wh . . . what's going on?"

"I'll tell you what's going on, honey!" exclaimed Pumpkin. "You didn't wake me up this morning. That's what's going on. But something woke me up. Do you know what that something was?"

"N . . . no."

"Hunger! That's what! My belly was rumbling so loud, I thought it was an earthquake. And do you know why I'm so hungry, honey?"

"N . . . no."

"Because it's four o'clock in the afternoon, honey! That's why! Four o'clock in the afternoon and no breakfast. I call, 'Honey!' But does my honey come with my pot of tea and boiled egg? No! And then I look at my bedside cabinet, and what do I see? Or rather, what don't I see?"

"W . . . what?"

"My brooch! That's what! Where is it, honey? You promised me you'd find it!"

Good heavens! thought Kasper. I don't believe it! I went all the way to the City to get the brooch and then forgot to ask Heartthrob for it.

"Pumpkin," said Kasper. "I'm so sorry. I searched . . . I searched all night. That's why I overslept. But I'll find it tonight. I promise!"

"I hope so, honey! This is the most unsparkling start to any day I've ever had. No breakfast, no brooch, and— Wait a minute!" She pulled the sheets from Kasper. "Honey! You're wearing your suit! Look at it! It's as creased as a concertina. I've never seen you look so unsparkling!"

Good heavens! thought Kasper. I must have just crawled into bed without taking my clothes off.

"Don't worry, Pumpkin," he said, getting out of bed. "Look! I'm up now! Why don't you just go back to bed while I go downstairs and make breakfast for you. Go on!" He kissed Pumpkin on the cheek. "Things'll soon start sparkling again."

"I hope so, honey," said Pumpkin. And she went back to her bedroom.

Kasper went downstairs to the kitchen. His muscles ached and he was still tired, but he knew he had to cheer Pumpkin up. He put an egg in a saucepan of water and filled the kettle. Then he sat at the kitchen table and waited for the water to boil.

Kasper's mind was full of the Gloom. There was a melon pip stuck to his jacket and he picked it off, re-membering all the fun he'd had with Heartthrob and Hushabye. Kasper couldn't bring himself to throw the melon pip away, so he put it in his pocket.

And he sat there thinking of quiffs and angels—

"Honey!"

—black eyes and bones—

"Wake up, honey!"

—tattoos and moths—

"WAKE UP, HONEY!"

Kasper's eyes clicked open.

Pumpkin was shaking him.

"Wh . . . what's going on?" he asked, rubbing his eyes.

"I'll tell you what's going on!" Pumpkin exclaimed. "I was upstairs waiting for the breakfast you promised to bring me, when, suddenly, what do I smell? Smoke! That's what!"

It was then Kasper realized the kitchen was full of smoke. He coughed and rushed to open a window.

"So I came down here!" continued Pumpkin. "And what do I see? You asleep at the table, and the saucepan burning on the stove! Honestly, honey, what's wrong with you today? Look at the ceiling. It's covered in soot! And the saucepan's ruined."

"I . . . I'm so tired from last night," said Kasper. "I'm sorry, Pumpkin. It won't happen again."

"I need a Banoffi pie, honey," Pumpkin declared. "Make me the best one you've ever made. That's the only thing that can help dispel this feeling of dullness that's creeping up all around me."

And, with that, she went back to her bedroom and started putting her makeup on.

Good heavens! thought Kasper. Banoffi pie! I don't want to make Banoffi pie. It reminds me of King Streetwise . . . but I've got to! For Pumpkin!

He put the ingredients on the table. Just looking at the bananas and toffee brought back memories of King Streetwise. Kasper could hear that hissing voice go "Yum" over and over again. "Yum" it went as Kasper sliced the bananas. "Yum" it went as Kasper prepared the toffee.

When the pie was finished, he looked through the window at the City. It was dark now. The lights in the buildings were shimmering against the sky. Heartthrob and Hushabye, thought Kasper. I'll be seeing you soon.

"Look, honey!" cried Pumpkin, entering the room. "There's still soot on the ceiling! I thought you would have cleaned it off by now."

"But I was making the pie. . . . " began Kasper, controlling his anger.

"No marmalade!" cried Pumpkin, looking at the pie. "Where's the dollop of marmalade that gives the pie its much needed tang? Get the marmalade at once. After all, I did break a nail getting it yesterday."

Kasper put a dollop of marmalade on her slice of pie.

"And what about the soot, honey?"

Count to ten! thought Kasper. One, two, three—

"Ugh! Honey! What have you done? This is the worst pie I've ever tasted."

—four, five, six—

"The banana is too thick!"

—seven, eight—

"The toffee is too runny!"

—nine—

"And there are lumps in the cream!"

—nine and a half—

"UGH! As if I haven't suffered enough today! First you forget to wake me up, then you leave me to starve to death without breakfast, then you burn the kitchen—"

—nine and three quarters—

"And now you've made the most unsparkling Banoffi pie I've ever tasted. Honestly, honey, can't you do one little thing for me—"

"THAT'S IT!" snapped Kasper. "I'VE HAD ENOUGH! ALL YOU DO IS BOSS ME AROUND! DO THIS, HONEY! DO THAT, HONEY! WELL, I'VE HAD ENOUGH. FROM NOW ON, PUMPKIN, THINGS ARE GOING TO CHANGE. FROM NOW ON, YOU'RE GOING TO HELP ME WITH THE HOUSEWORK AND COOKING AND GARDENING. AND I WANT FRIENDS, PUMPKIN! YOU HEAR ME? FRIENDS!"

Pumpkin stared at Kasper. There was a glazed, horrified look in her eyes, as if she'd just experienced the most terrifying ghost train in the world.

Then she went: *Sob!*

But, this time, Kasper didn't say he was sorry.

Sob!

Still Kasper said nothing.

Slowly, Pumpkin stood up. "I'm going to bed now," she said in a broken voice.

Pumpkin went straight up to her bedroom. And, for the first time in Kasper's memory, she didn't stop and blow kisses on every step.

Good heavens! thought Kasper. Pumpkin's so upset! What have I done?

Sob!

Good heavens! She's asleep already! I can tell by the sound of her voice. And she's not calling "A facial!"

Sob!

She's crying in her sleep! And it's all my fault.

Sob!

Oh, Pumpkin! I'm so sorry I upset you!

Sob!

I never knew making friends would be this confusing!

And that's when he heard a gentle rapping at the front door.

And two familiar voices whispered through the mailbox.

"You in there, Brother Kasper?"

"It's us, man!"

K asper opened the door.

"Hello, Brother Kasper," said Hushabye. "We've been waiting out in the Nothing."

"Waiting for hours, man!"

"Don't exaggerate, Brother Heartthrob. It wasn't hours at all. As I said, we've been waiting in the Nothing for your mother to go to bed. And then I saw a light go on and off upstairs. I guessed that was her. Was I correct, Brother Kasper?"

"Er . . . yes."

"So it's safe to come in, Brother Kasper?"

Sob!

Kasper looked upstairs.

"What's wrong, Brother Kasper?" asked Hushabye.

"Pumpkin is sobbing in her sleep," he replied. "Can't you hear her?"

Hushabye and Heartthrob listened very hard.

"No, Brother Kasper."

"Hear what, man?"

"But how can you not hear it?" exclaimed Kasper. "It's deafening!"

"Don't worry about it, man! I'm sure she'll be fine. Besides, I've got my own problems to worry about! Look! My suntan's fading!"

"Well, you go to a sunbed, Brother Heartthrob. I need to talk to Brother Kasper about his garden."

Heartthrob rushed into the house.

"Now then, Brother Kasper," said Hushabye, pointing at a rosebush, "you've been pruning these all wrong."

Kasper looked up at Pumpkin's bedroom window. He found it hard to concentrate on anything, knowing she was crying.

"Brother Kasper?"

"Er . . . what?"

"The roses! You've been pruning them wrong. Look here! This is just silliness to prune them like this! You'd get twice as many blooms if you did it properly. Pay attention now—I'm trying to teach you something."

"Well, don't bother!" snapped Kasper. "Pumpkin teaches me all I need to know. And I don't like you finding fault with my garden!"

Kasper stormed into the house.

Heartthrob was under a sunbed.

"Thirsty work, man!"

"Er . . . what?"

"Where's my lemonade?"

"Get it yourself!" cried Kasper. "I'm not your servant!"

Sob!

Kasper looked upstairs.

"Brother Kasper's in a very touchy mood," said Hushabye, entering the salon. "Honestly, Brother Kasper, I thought we were invited out here. I thought we'd be welcome."

"You are welcome!" said Kasper. "But Pumpkin's crying and—"

"But what's she got to cry about, Brother Kasper? She's got a home, food, a warm bed. Crying is just silly—"

"It's not silly!" snapped Kasper. "I won't let you call Pumpkin silly! I'll tell you why she's crying. Because I told her I wanted friends, that's why!"

"And here we are, Brother Kasper. Your friends."

Sob!

"Oh, Pumpkin!" cried Kasper, looking upstairs. "Pumpkin!" He looked at Hushabye and Heartthrob. "I can't bear to think of Pumpkin upset! You hear me? I just can't bear it. And . . . well, the other night, when I met Heartthrob, I . . . I thought I wanted friends—"

Sob!

"What are you trying to say, Brother Kasper?"

"What I'm trying to say is . . . I want things to be just as they were before I met Heartthrob. When it was just me and Pumpkin."

Hushabye took a step forward and stared at Kasper. "Let me get this right, Brother Kasper," she said. "You want us to go. Is that right?"

Kasper nodded.

"Go!" exclaimed Heartthrob, getting off the sunbed. "You mean go and never come back?"

Again, Kasper nodded.

"But . . . but what about the sunbed, man?"

"No more sunbed," Kasper told him softly.

"Put your jacket on, Brother Heartthrob. Brother Kasper wants us to go. I'm not one to stay where I'm not wanted."

Heartthrob hesitated, then put his jacket on. He looked at Kasper. "Well . . . bye, man," he said.

"Good-bye," said Kasper, looking at the floor.

"Good-bye, Brother Kasper."

"G . . . good-bye."

Heartthrob and Hushabye walked towards the door.

And then they stopped.

Because a new sound had filled the air.

A distant rattling!

A distant howling!

"I know those sounds," said Hushabye.

"Me too, man."

They peered into the Nothing.

Something was gleaming in the dark.

Gleaming gold and getting closer.

"No," Kasper whispered. "It can't be!"

King Streetwise was in his Chariot, flicking his whip in the air, followed by the Argonauts, and heading straight for the Sparkle Plenty house.

"HUSHABYE!" King Streetwise roared. "I LOVE YOU!"

Kasper slammed the front door shut.

"He's as silly as ever," Hushabye said irritably.

"The rose petals!" cried Kasper. "He must have found your hiding place, then followed the trail of rose petals from the other night."

The rattling and howling got louder and louder.

"What are we going to do?" asked Heartthrob.

"I'm not sure, Brother Heartthrob," replied Hushabye. "We seem to be trapped."

"My quiff!" cried Heartthrob. He was trembling with fear. His blue eyes were very wide, and his lips were quivering. "He'll make me wear a helmet and ruin my quiff!"

Outside, the noise of the approaching Chariot was getting so loud that the very ground seemed to be quaking.

Heartthrob started to back down the hall. "My quiff!" he said in a petrified whisper. "My quiff! My quiff!"

"Please, Brother Heartthrob," said Hushabye, grabbing hold of his arm. "Don't panic—"

Smash!

A brick crashed through a kitchen window!

Heartthrob screamed.

"They . . . they're . . . attacking the house!" Kasper gasped in disbelief. "Actually attacking!"

Smash!

Another brick!

This time through a salon window.

It crashed into one of the sunbeds.

Bang! went the sunbed as one of the lamps exploded.

Sparks and broken glass filled the room.

Heartthrob screamed again.

"I LOVE YOU, HUSHABYE!" boomed the King's voice from outside. "I LOVE YOU!"

Smash!

Another window.

Fragments of glass landed at Kasper's feet.

And then the lights went out!

M y quiff!" cried Heart-
throb in the darkness. "Don't touch my quiff." And, suddenly, he was running to the back of the house. "My quiff
. . . my quiff!"

"Keep calm!" urged Hushabye.

But Heartthrob opened the back door and rushed outside.

Hushabye chased after him.

And then . . .

A knocking on the front door!

"LET ME IN, HUSHABYE!" came the King's voice.

Kasper peered through the dark at the door.

The King knocked again.

"I WANT TO SEE YOUR PRETTY HAIR."

Kasper was too scared to move. It was as if his feet
were glued to the carpet.

"Knock the door down, Argonauts," Kasper heard the
King say.

And that's what they started to do.

Bang!

The door shook.

Bang!

Hinges creaked.

Bang!

Wood splintered.

I've got to hide, thought Kasper.

But still he couldn't move.

Bang!

A large crack appeared down the middle of the door.
Moonlight shone through the crack.

Bang!

They'll knock it down any second now, thought
Kasper.

Bang!

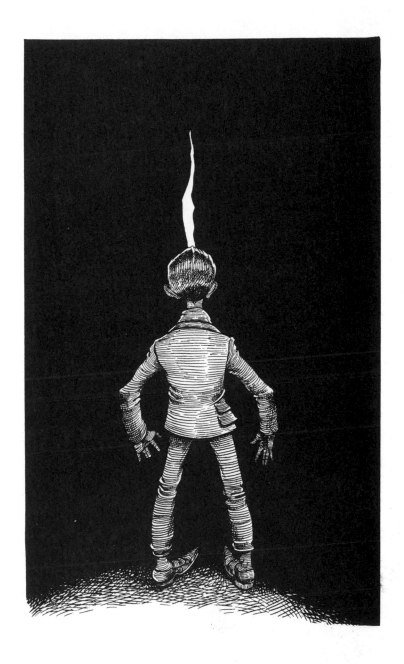

And then, through the widening crack, he saw something gleaming.
Gold!

It was King Streetwise's cloak!

The sight of it jolted Kasper into movement.

He ran to the cupboard beneath the stairs and scampered inside.

And just in time, too. Because, as Kasper closed the cupboard door behind him, there was an almighty *bang!* and the front door crashed to the ground.

The cupboard was full of toys: a miniature car, a toy robot, and a doll's house. There was also a small tin bath that Pumpkin used to wash him in when he was a baby.

Kasper climbed into the tin bath now, then piled the toys on top of him to hide himself.

Footsteps could be heard in the house as the King and the Argonauts rushed in.

"I LOVE YOU, HUSHABYE!" called the King. "WHERE ARE YOU?"

There were tiny cracks in the cupboard door. Shadows moved against these cracks as the King and the Argonauts moved about outside.

"Where is she, squires?"

"Search everywhere, old beans."

"Every corner, chiefs."

"Woof, mateys!"

"I LOVE YOU, HUSHABYE!" Streetwise roared.

His voice was louder than ever.

The King was standing right outside the cupboard.

The cracks glinted gold.

Kasper held his breath.

"TEAR IT!" shrieked the King angrily. "TEAR IT ALL TO PIECES."

Sounds of ripping and tearing and smashing filled the air.

Kasper couldn't bear it.

But what could he do? There was only one of him. He didn't stand a chance against them.

Crash!

Smash!

Bang!

Rip!

Kasper put his fingers in his ears and closed his eyes very tight.

And, in his world of silent dark, he murmured, "Go away! Go away! Go away!"

37

*K*asper opened his eyes.

Darkness.

He took his fingers from his ears.

Silence.

He wasn't sure how long he'd been hiding in the toy cupboard. Fear had made him lose all sense of time. But the silence told him one thing: King Streetwise had gone.

Slowly, he pushed the toys aside, crawled out of the tin bath, and opened the cupboard door.

And his fear was replaced by shock!

It was as if a whirlwind had hit the house.

All the lights had been smashed or broken, so the only illumination was the moonlight. And in this moonlight Kasper saw . . .

Wallpaper torn from walls.

Curtains yanked from windows.

Carpets pulled from floorboards.

Kasper walked into the kitchen, his feet crunching over shattered glass and crockery.

Cupboards had been smashed.

Food was splattered up the walls and across the floor.

The gas cooker was buckled, its door ripped off.

Kasper glanced through the broken window to look at the garden outside.

Or, rather, what was left of it!

The once-beautiful rosebushes had been totally ruined. There was nothing left but a trampled mass of twigs and branches. One or two bushes had even been dug up and thrown into the house.

Kasper went to the beauty salon.

The hair dryers had been ripped from the walls. All the magazines had been torn to shreds. The sunbeds had been broken beyond repair.

All except one.

Suddenly, it flickered on!

And, in the dazzling light, Kasper saw a face. . . .

eartthrob!" gasped Kasper.

Heartthrob was curled in a corner, his face buried in his hands.

"The King got Hushabye, man," Heartthrob said. "And it's all my fault!"

"No—" Kasper began.

"It is!" snapped Heartthrob, looking up. "I ran away. Hushabye was right. I'm nothing but a scaredy-cat Heart-throb."

"Tell . . . tell me what happened," said Kasper. "How did the King catch Hushabye?"

"It all happened so quickly, man," replied Heartthrob. "I ran out into the Nothing. I didn't know where I was going. I panicked! I could hear Hushabye calling out behind me. But . . . I was too scared to slow down or turn around. Then . . . then I stumbled over. And I just lay there. I don't know how long for. And then . . ." His voice trailed away.

"And then?" asked Kasper.

"I looked back . . ." he said. "And I saw the King with Hushabye. She was wrapped in sheets. She was screaming. The King threw her in the back of the Chariot and drove away. The Argonauts were cheering. . . ." Heartthrob buried his face in his hands. "I should have been braver," he said. "I should have . . . helped in some way."

Kasper sat beside Heartthrob and put his arm around his shoulder.

"I'm just as much to blame," Kasper said.

"How can you be, man?"

Kasper took a deep breath, then replied, "It was me who told the King where to find you."

"When?"

"When I was at the Palace."

"But why, man?"

"I didn't know what I was doing at the time, Heartthrob. Honestly. Last night the King attacked the wrong bridge. But tonight he got the right one. I'm sorry."

They sat in silence for a while.

The sunbed flickered off and on, off and on.

Then . . .

Footsteps!

Heartthrob and Kasper jumped to their feet.

"Who's there?" cried Kasper.

And that's when someone walked into the salon.

I t's me, Brother Heartthrob," said Hushabye. "Thank goodness you're both safe," she said.

"But . . . but . . ." stammered Heartthrob.

"But what, Brother Heartthrob?"

"You can't be here!"

"Why not?"

"Because you chased after me," said Heartthrob, "and I fell over and—"

"And I couldn't find my way back," Hushabye said. "I must have run farther than I thought. And without the lights on, the house was very difficult to find, Brother Heartthrob."

"But the King got you!" cried Heartthrob. "I saw him throw you in the back of the Chariot."

"Not me," Hushabye said.

"Then who?" asked Heartthrob.

And, suddenly, something occurred to Kasper.

"Oh, no!" he cried. "No!"

And he ran out of the salon, up the stairs, and into Pumpkin's bedroom.

The room had been wrecked.

Sheets pulled from the bed.

The empty bed!

"NO!" shrieked Kasper.

He ran back down the stairs.

"He's got my mother!" he yelled. "The King has taken my mother!"

And he ran out of the house, through the remains of the garden, and into the wasteland.

"GIVE ME BACK MY PUMPKIN!" he screamed. "GIVE ME BACK MY PUMPKIN!"

*H*is screams turned to cries. . . .

Then sobs . . .

Then moans . . .

Heartthrob and Hushabye tried to comfort him. But he took no notice. He just gazed at the stars and chanted Pumpkin's name over and over again.

Finally, though, the chanting stopped and Kasper got to his feet.

He looked at his house: at the ruined garden and broken windows. Even the neon SPARKLE PLENTY sign had been smashed, showering the trampled garden with glass. Through one shattered window, the flashing light of the sunbed could be seen.

"I've got to save Pumpkin," Kasper said, his eyes flashing with sunbed light.

"But you can't, man!" exclaimed Heartthrob. "There's only three of us."

"Brother Heartthrob is right," agreed Hushabye. "It won't be sensible. It's not just the King we'll have to face, after all."

"There's Skinnybones," Heartthrob reminded him.

"And Poodlecut," said Hushabye.

"And Fingerpoppin."

"And Knucklehead."

"And Jingo."

"Not to mention Moonglow."

"And Stardust," said Hushabye, completing the list. "No, Brother Kasper," she continued. "It won't be sensible unless we have a plan—"

"But I've got a plan," interrupted Kasper.

"I bet it's dangerous, though," said Heartthrob.

"But is it sensible?" asked Hushabye. "That's the main thing."

"It's probably very dangerous and very unsensible," Kasper told them. "But it might also get us into the Palace and cause enough confusion to not only save Pumpkin but also teach the King a lesson he'll never forget."

Heartthrob and Hushabye just stared at him.

A gentle breeze blew petals and leaves around their feet.

"Listen to me," Kasper said, his voice getting louder. "The King is going to keep on forcing people to be his friend. And now . . . now he's actually kidnapping. Or, rather, Pumpkin-napping. Soon no child will be safe to walk the streets without King Streetwise tempting them to join him in the Gloom." His voice got louder still. "We can't just hide away and do nothing," he cried, the light from the sunbed blazing in his eyes. "We've got to do something!"

"You're right, Brother Kasper," said Hushabye. "I've done nothing for too long. Of course I'll help you."

"Thank you," said Kasper. Then looked at Heartthrob.

"I don't know, man," Heartthrob said. "What if King Streetwise cuts off my quiff—"

"What's your plan, Brother Kasper?" Hushabye interrupted, ignoring Heartthrob.

"We'll have to move fast," said Kasper. "There's a tin bathtub in the cupboard beneath the stairs. We need that. Come and help me."

Kasper and Hushabye went to get the bathtub.

"What now?" asked Hushabye.

"I want you to start taping pages of these magazines together," Kasper said. "I know most of them have been torn, but we need enough stuck together to cover the top of the tub."

"Like the skin on a drum?"

"Exactly."

"Then what?"

"You'll see," said Kasper.

He found some tape and gave it to Hushabye.

While Hushabye stuck pages together, Kasper rummaged in the rubble for a few tins of cream, packets of chocolate granules, and a jar of marmalade.

"Is this big enough, Brother Kasper?" Hushabye asked, when she'd taped together as many magazine pages as she could find.

"I think so," he replied. "Let's see."

And they stretched the paper over the top of the tin bathtub.

"Just right!" said Kasper.

They stuck the edge of the paper around the rim of the tub until it resembled (as Hushabye had said) a drum.

"Now what, Brother Kasper?" asked Hushabye, getting excited by the whole thing.

"I'm going to spread a very thin layer of cream on top

of the paper," Kasper told her. "Then put chocolate flakes and a spoonful of marmalade on the top."

"Why?" asked Hushabye.

"Because then it will look like a very big Banoffi pie."

"But there won't be any pie inside."

"That's right."

"So how will it help us, Brother Kasper?"

"Because," said Kasper, "before I cover the paper with cream, I'm going to make a tiny hole in it." He stuck his finger through the paper. "Now through this hole I'm going to put—"

"Moths!" said a voice.

They turned.

Heartthrob stood in the doorway.

"Am I right or am I right?" he asked.

"You're right," Kasper said. "Moths it is!"

"And we'll take the pie to Streetwise and say we're sorry for running away. And when he goes to eat—moths will fly out. And he'll become a scaredy-cat. Am I right or am I right?"

"You're right," Kasper said.

"And while he's being a scaredy-cat, we'll rescue Pumpkin. Am I right or am I right?"

"You're right," said Kasper.

"And we'll torment him with the moths until he promises to leave children alone," said Heartthrob. "Am I right or am I right?"

"You're right," said Kasper.

Heartthrob stepped into the kitchen. "There's something . . . you have to know," he said. "About Streetwise."

"What?" asked Kasper.

"Well . . . you see, man, Streetwise . . . is . . ."

"Is what?"

"My brother," said Heartthrob.

Your brother?" exclaimed Kasper.

Heartthrob nodded.

"Did you know?" Kasper asked Hushabye.

"Yes, Brother Kasper," Hushabye replied. "But Brother Heartthrob never wanted to talk about it. And as it was his secret to tell . . . well, I didn't think it was my place to say anything."

Kasper looked at Heartthrob. "So both you and Streetwise once had a home then," he said.

"Yes, man."

"With a mum?"

"Yes, man. And a dad. And . . . I was happy there."

"So why did you run away?" asked Kasper.

"Because Streetwise persuaded me, of course!" cried Heartthrob. "Ever since I can remember, Streetwise has hated mums and dads and all that stuff. You know what my earliest memory is?"

"What?"

"Me laying in my cradle, and Streetwise looking down at me and saying 'Yuck'!"

Kasper shivered at the thought of it.

"Streetwise is older than me, don't forget," Heartthrob went on. "Every night, before we went to sleep, he'd start talking to me about how exciting the Gloom was. How we should run away. One night, he did it. He ran away. I managed to resist going with him that time."

"That's when Streetwise met Hushabye."

"Spot on, man. Obviously Streetwise wasn't as good at living in the Gloom as he thought he'd be. Not if he was cold and hungry when he met Hushabye. But . . . Hushabye taught him."

"Don't remind me, Brother Heartthrob."

"And then what?" asked Kasper. "Did Streetwise come back for you?"

"Spot on, man."

"And this time he persuaded you to run away."

"Spot on, man."

"And you couldn't resist," said Kasper.

"I couldn't help it, man! He told me the Gloom was the best place in the universe. That he was going to be the King of the Gloom. That he'd found his Queen—"

"Silly boy!" snapped Hushabye.

"And that, if I ran away, I'd be an Argonaut and share in his glory. And . . . and I believed him. So I ran away. . . ." Tears appeared in Heartthrob's eyes. "We've . . . we've got to stop him!" exclaimed Heartthrob, brushing the tears aside. "Stop Streetwise!"

"Bravo, Brother Heartthrob!" cried Hushabye, clapping her hands excitedly.

"Now let's catch those moths!" said Heartthrob. "I used to catch moths to torment Streetwise with when we lived at home. It was the only way I could get him to shut up some nights. So I'm an expert at it. Come on, you two, we've got children to save!"

Because of the flashing sunbed, lots of moths had been attracted to the salon.

One by one, Heartthrob and Hushabye caught them and put them through the hole in the paper and into the bathtub.

Kasper counted them as they went in.

"One . . . two . . . three . . ."

More and more moths.

" . . . twenty . . . twenty-one . . ."

More and more.

" . . . thirty-eight . . ."

More.

" . . . fifty-six . . ."

More.

" . . . seventy-eight . . ."

"How many more?" asked Heartthrob.

"Let's make it a round hundred," replied Kasper, grinning.

And that's what they did!

When the hundred moths were in the tub, Kasper sealed the hole up with some tape, then carefully spread the cream over the paper.

"Be careful, Brother Kasper," warned Hushabye. "Otherwise the paper will break."

"I know," Kasper said. "But, luckily, magazine paper is very tough."

Once the cream was on top, Kasper sprinkled on the chocolate granules, got the marmalade, and put a large spoonful in the middle.

"There!" exclaimed Kasper. "The biggest Banoffi pie in the universe!"

Heartthrob and Hushabye giggled with excitement.

There was a handle on each side of the bathtub.

Carefully, Kasper and Hushabye picked it up.

They could hear the moths flapping around inside.

Kasper looked at them both. "I want you to know," he said, "no matter what happens . . . you two are the best friends anyone could have."

"I feel the same, Brother Kasper."

"Me too, man."

"And now . . . let's teach the King a lesson," said Kasper.

"TO SAVE ALL THE CHILDREN IN THE WORLD!"
cried Heartthrob.

"TO SAVE ALL THE CHILDREN IN THE WORLD!"
cried Hushabye.

"TO SAVE ALL THE CHILDREN IN THE WORLD!"
cried Kasper.

Part 3

KASPER THE SAVED

I'm getting scared now,"
Kasper mumbled to himself.

"What did you say, Brother Kasper?" asked Hushabye.

"Oh—I'm sorry. I've got so used to talking to myself. I just said I'm getting a little scared now. Seeing the Palace again."

"Yes, Brother Kasper," sighed Hushabye. "I know how you feel."

Kasper and Hushabye (still holding the bathtub) and Heartthrob stood at the end of the deserted street, looking at the Palace.

A full moon shone behind the building.

"And just look what he's done to my bushes," said Hushabye, stamping her foot angrily. "Not a rose in sight."

"I should have warned you," said Kasper. "Streetwise got Skinnybones to cut them off and frazzle them because they reminded him of you."

"Oh, what silliness," said Hushabye. "You know, Brother Kasper, there's such silliness on the planet, sometimes I wonder how it stays in orbit."

They started to walk towards the Palace.

All they could hear were their footsteps, their beating hearts, and the moths inside the tub.

As they reached the path leading up to the Palace's door, however, another sound filled the air.

It was a gentle weeping.

It was coming from the top of the steeple.

"It's Pumpkin!" Kasper gasped. "She's up there! Oh, no!" He went to rush forward.

"Careful, Brother Kasper!" warned Hushabye. "We'll drop the pie!"

"But listen to Pumpkin!" exclaimed Kasper. "She sounds so upset and scared."

"And we're going to rescue her!" Hushabye assured him. "But only if we do one thing at a time. First we've got to get into the Palace. Then Streetwise has got to start eating the pie. And then—"

"Moths!" Heartthrob finished gleefully.

They walked down the path and up to the wooden door.

"Please knock, Brother Heartthrob," said Hushabye.

Heartthrob went to knock, then paused. He looked at the others. "Tell me something," he said. "Are you two as scared as me?"

"I should think so," said Hushabye.

"Most certainly," said Kasper.

The news seemed to please Heartthrob. "That's good," he said. "At least I'm not the only one." Then he knocked on the door.

The sound reverberated inside.

Kasper glanced at Hushabye. She gave him a reassuring smile.

Heartthrob was shaking so much, his quiff was wobbling.

They all jumped when the door opened.

Jingo stood there, brushing his jacket tails. One of his eyes was black and very swollen.

"Gracious me!" he said, peering at them with his good eye. "Master Kasper! And Master Heartthrob. And . . . is that you, Mistress Hushabye?"

"Yes, Brother Jingo," Hushabye said.

"But your pretty hair has—"

"Gone!" interrupted Hushabye firmly. "And if you say *pretty* one more time, I'll give you another black eye."

Jingo touched his swollen eye and winced. "We've all got black eyes tonight," he said. "We went in search of you, you see."

"I know, Brother Jingo," Hushabye said. "But the Argonauts got Kasper's mother instead. Right?"

Jingo nodded.

"I knew they were silly," Hushabye said. "But not *that* silly."

"Oh, if you'll permit me," Jingo said. "It wasn't all their fault. After all, they were looking for your pretty—"

Hushabye raised a clenched fist in the air.

"I'm sorry," offered Jingo, nervously flinching back. He took a deep breath and continued. "They were looking for your hair!" he said. "And, also, the King had given us all a black eye the night before because we let Master Kasper get away. So they were half-blind, so to speak."

"Poor Poodlecut had a black eye anyway," said Kasper.

"Well, he's got two now," Jingo said. "In fact, they've all got two. As I say, the King hit them again tonight when they took your mother instead of Hushabye."

"Silly, silly, silly!" Hushabye said angrily, stamping her foot every time she said the word. Then she indicated the tin tub. "We've brought Streetwise the biggest Banoffi pie in the world. It's a gift. We want to swap it for Pumpkin."

"Thank goodness," sighed Jingo. "That should put him in a good mood. I'll let him know you're here."

Jingo went back inside and closed the door.

Noises could be heard from inside the Palace.

Whispering voices.

Rushing footsteps.

Growling dogs.

And one loud "YUM!" from King Streetwise.

The sound of his voice startled all three of them.

"He won't be saying that when he sees what's inside the pie," said Hushabye.

Kasper and Heartthrob grinned in agreement.

The next second, Jingo opened the door again. He was about to speak when a voice bellowed from inside the Palace, "ENTER, MY MOONLIT DUDES."

King Streetwise was sitting in the Throne.

Moonglow and Stardust sat on either side. Eyes wide and red. Saliva dribbling from their fangs.

The Argonauts stood in the shadows behind.

"I think it's Kasper, squires."

"And Heartthrob, old beans."

"With Hushabye, chiefs."

"Woof, mateys."

Candlelight flickered everywhere.

King Streetwise was wearing his golden cloak. It shot out beams of light in all directions.

The King's eyes grew wide with horror when he saw Hushabye's bald head.

Slowly, Kasper, Hushabye, and Heartthrob walked down the aisle towards him.

The dogs snarled louder.

Kasper's heart thumped like a sledgehammer in his chest.

The Argonauts were muttering in the shadows.

"Can you see them, squires?"

"No, old bean. Can you?"

"No, chiefs."

"Woof, mateys."

"Shut up, you idiotic dudes!" snapped Streetwise. And his voice echoed around the Palace. "You don't want to see what I can see. Well—hey there!—it's the saddest sight in the history of sad sights. My beloved Hushabye has done something terrible to her pretty hair."

Kasper saw Hushabye clench her teeth in anger. But she didn't say anything.

Good, thought Kasper. We've got to keep calm. Nothing must get in the way of the plan.

The Argonauts started mumbling in the shadows again.

"What's she done to her hair, squires?"

"Has she dyed it, old beans?"

"Or permed it, chiefs?"

"Or woofed it, mateys?"

"SHUT UP!" yelled Streetwise again. "My beautiful Hushabye has shaved her hair off. She's bald!"

"Bald, squires!"

"Not a hair, old beans."

"An egghead, chiefs."

"Woof, mateys."

Kasper and Hushabye put the tin tub in front of the throne.

Then stepped back and looked at Streetwise.

"Well—hey there!—and yum!" murmured Streetwise, sniffing the pie. "Oh, yum, yum, yum!" He looked at Kasper. "Is this your way of saying sorry?" he asked. "Sorry for running away?"

"Absolutely," replied Kasper softly.

"And—hey there!—am I still your best friend?"

"Certainly."

Streetwise smiled and nodded. Then he looked at Heartthrob.

"You were such a disappointment to me," he said. "My own brother running away with my greatest love. What a yucky moonlit dude you turned out to be."

Heartthrob didn't say anything.

Streetwise stood up.

"And so . . ." he said, still looking at Heartthrob, "before I eat this wonderful pie, you're going to do something for me."

Streetwise walked into the shadows where the Argonauts stood.

"Something to show me how sorry you are for what you did," said Streetwise from the darkness.

When King Streetwise came out of the shadows, he was holding a golden helmet in one hand, and had his other hand behind his back.

Heartthrob started to tremble. "No . . ." he said softly.

Kasper shot him a look.

The look said: Don't forget the plan! We've got to make sure King Streetwise eats the pie!

Streetwise approached Heartthrob.

"Don't make me wear the helmet," pleaded Heartthrob. "It'll ruin my quiff."

"Well—hey there!—I wouldn't want the helmet to do that," said Streetwise. "That's why"—he brought his other hand from behind his back, and it was holding a pair of scissors—"it's time for a haircut!"

Snip-snip went the scissors.

"No!" whimpered Heartthrob. "Don't cut off my quiff!"

"Well—hey there!—*I'm* not going to cut if off," said Streetwise, handing the scissors to Heartthrob. "*You* are!"

Heartthrob looked at the scissors.

He was trembling, his eyes full of fear, his quiff wobbling.

Kasper glanced at Hushabye.

She shook her head sadly.

There was nothing they could do: The dogs were watching them, growling. If they made a sudden move to break open the top of the pie, the dogs might attack them before they got there. And then the plan would be ruined.

"Cut off the quiff!" said Streetwise, glaring at Heartthrob.

Heartthrob didn't move.

"Do it!" hissed Streetwise.

Slowly, Heartthrob raised the scissors to his hair.

He paused.

"Do it!" hissed Streetwise.

Heartthrob looked at Kasper and Hushabye.

The silver blades of the scissors were touching his black hair.

Kasper offered a sympathetic smile.

So did Hushabye.

"DO IT!" roared Streetwise.

And then, a new look filled Heartthrob's eyes. The fear disappeared and was replaced by something colder. An ice-cold rage. And then . . .

Snip!

Heartthrob started cutting his hair.

"Yum!" cried

Streetwise, spinning around and around. "Yum, yum, yum!"

Snip-snip!

The Argonauts muttered.

"Is he doing it, squires?"

"He can't be, old beans!"

"Not his precious quiff, chiefs!"

"Woof, mateys!"

"HE IS!" yelled Streetwise into the shadows. "Heartthrob is cutting off his perfect quiff!"

Snip, snip, snip.

More and more hair tumbled to the floor.

Kasper and Hushabye had to look away.

But there was no expression on Heartthrob's face.

Just that cold rage.

When all the quiff had been cut off, Heartthrob gave the scissors back to Streetwise.

"Look at you!" sneered Streetwise, when all the quiff had been cut off. "How totally ugly you look." He snatched the scissors from Heartthrob. "People will laugh if they see you quiffless. So"—slowly, he put the golden helmet on Heartthrob's head—"let's cover it with this. There! You're an Argonaut after all!"

Heartthrob just glared at Streetwise from beneath the rim of the helmet.

"And now . . ." said Streetwise, turning to Hushabye, "it's your turn."

"I've got no hair to cut off!" Hushabye said.

"I can see that," said Streetwise. "But you're going to do something else for me?"

"What?"

"TELL ME YOU LOVE ME!" demanded the King. "NOW!"

*H*ushabye glanced at Kasper.

He knew she had no choice but to do as the King asked.

"Say it!" cried Streetwise.

A pause.

And then . . . from the shadows they heard a muttering.

It was Poodlecut.

"What's that noise, old bean?" he was asking. "Is it a moth?"

Poodlecut—with his keen hearing—had heard the moths in the tin tub.

Good heavens, thought Kasper. Our plan's going to be ruined unless Hushabye says it. And says it quickly. But she doesn't want to. I can tell from the look on her face. She doesn't want to lie about something like that.

"Say it!" Streetwise demanded.

Hushabye's lips started twitching.

"Say it!"

Twitching.

"Say it!"

"What's that noise, old bean?" asked Poodlecut again.

"I'm sure it's a moth! More than one!"

Kasper's eyes pleaded with Hushabye: Please say it! Please! For the sake of the plan! For the sake of all the children in the world.

"I . . ." Hushabye began. Her voice was a barely audible croak.

"Yes?" encouraged Streetwise.

"I . . ."

"What's that noise, old bean?"

"SAY IT!"

Twitching.

Please say it! thought Kasper. You have to!

And then he saw that Hushabye wasn't looking at King Streetwise. She was looking at him. At Kasper.

"I love you," she said.

"Louder!" demanded Streetwise.

"I LOVE YOU!" yelled Hushabye, still looking at Kasper.

Kasper looked back and smiled.

Streetwise went back to the throne.

"What's that noise—?" began Poodlecut.

"Be quiet back there," snapped the King. "It's time for my pie."

And he raised one hand into the air.

Kasper watched.

Any minute now the hand would plunge down and—

"Do it!" hissed Kasper under his breath. "Eat!"

"Well—hey there!—YUM!" roared Streetwise.

And stuck his hand into the pie!

A moth flew out.

Streetwise screamed.

Then another moth.

Another scream.

More moths.

"Gracious me!" exclaimed Jingo.

"YUCK!" yelled Streetwise. "MOTHS! YUCK! YUCK!" He jumped back, trying to shield himself from the moths.

Suddenly, the moths were everywhere.

All one hundred of them erupted from the hole in the pie.

"What's going on, squires?"

"He said moths, old beans! I knew I could hear one!"

"Sounds like a real squabble, chiefs."

"Woof, mateys."

And the Argonauts stepped out of the shadows.

It was only then that Kasper realized why they were asking so many questions. With their eyes so black and swollen, the Argonauts couldn't see! If they'd been half-blind the night before, then they were totally blind now.

Streetwise was still screaming.

He rushed around the Palace.

And everywhere he went, there were more moths.

And everywhere he went, he knocked over candles.

The candles fell amongst the broken wood of the pews.

The wood began to smoulder.

Then burn.

"Gracious me!" exclaimed Jingo. "Here we go again!"

For a moment, Kasper was so taken aback by all the commotion that he couldn't move. He just stood there (with Heartthrob and Hushabye) and watched Streetwise.

But when he saw the wood catch fire, he clicked into action.

"Jingo!" he cried. "There's too many fires! The place will start to burn soon. We've got to help the Argonauts out. They can't see."

"Come on, Master Kasper! I'll help you! We've got to move fast."

Flames were erupting from all corners of the Palace now.

Black smoke began to fill the building.

And more candles were falling.

And more wood was burning.

Kasper went to speak to Heartthrob.

But Heartthrob was gone!

He looked all around.

And then he saw . . .

Heartthrob was chasing after Streetwise. "You made me cut my quiff off! My fuse is well and truly blown now! I'm gonna give *you* a black eye!" Heartthrob clenched his fist.

"Don't hurt me!" Streetwise whimpered. "Please!" He flinched as a moth flew nearby. "Help!" he cried, his voice trembling.

Heartthrob got closer.

Streetwise started to cry.

"What's that noise, squires?"

"Sounds like crying, old bean."

"Uncool blubbering it is, chiefs."

"But who—woof—is it, mateys?"

"It's Brother Streetwise," Hushabye told them, helping them out of the Palace. "He's blubbering like a baby. You see what a silly bully and coward he really is. Honestly! I've seen gelatin braver than him! Now, come on, you lot. Out this way! Through the door! Brother Jingo, mind your jacket on that burning wood there!"

"Gracious me! Thank you, Mistress Hushabye."

Hushabye and Jingo led the Argonauts out of the Palace.

Kasper could hear the Argonauts muttering. . . .

"Streetwise is a coward, squires."

"And a bully, old bean."

"What uncool idiots we were to follow him, chiefs."

"Woof, mateys!"

And then Streetwise rushed out of the Palace, calling, "Help me, Argonauts! Help me!"

"They won't help you now, man!" cried Heartthrob, chasing after him. "Nothing's gonna stop me giving you a black eye! It's the only thing that'll unblow my fuse."

Kasper was alone in the burning Palace now.

Time to save Pumpkin, he thought.

Kasper darted between the flames.

He ran toward the stairs that led to the steeple.

"I'm here, Pumpkin!" he called.

He started to climb the stairs as quickly as he could.

Smoke and sparks followed him.

"Pumpkin! Pumpkin!"

"Honey!"

When Kasper got to the top of the steeple, he looked around frantically.

At first he couldn't see her.

But he could hear her.

"Honey! Oh, honey!"

"Where are you, Pumpkin?"

"Honey!"

And then he saw!

Pumpkin was under the bell!

Only her head was visible, sticking out of the hole at the top.

Kasper rushed up to her.

He was gleaming with sweat now.

"Honey!"

Pumpkin's eyes were wide with fear, her face begrimed with dirt.

"Honey!"

"Are you all right, Pumpkin?"

Pumpkin was too scared to do anything but stare and tremble and say, "Honey!"

Kasper bent down and slipped his fingers under the bottom of the bell.

He tried to raise it.

But the bell was far too heavy.

"I need help!" cried Kasper.

He looked out one of the openings.

Hushabye and Jingo had shepherded the Argonauts to the other side of the street. The two dogs—Moonglow and Stardust—were beside Knucklehead. They looked as harmless as puppies now.

"Hushabye!" yelled Kasper.

Hushabye looked up at the spire.

"Help me!" Kasper cried.

"Be right there, Brother Kasper!"

Hushabye rushed back into the Palace.

Kasper went to the top of the stairs to wait for her.

A lot of smoke was billowing up.

The air was full of the stench of burning.

Kasper could hear Hushabye coughing below.

He went down a few steps.

And then he saw . . .

Several steps were on fire!

"Run!" called Kasper. "Quick!"

He heard Hushabye's footsteps.

"Quick!" he urged again.

Then he saw her!

Her face was black with soot, her eyes red-rimmed and watery.

She glanced up at him.

"Oh, Brother Kasper—" she spluttered.

And that's when the stairs collapsed.

And Hushabye started to fall!

AHHHHH!" screamed Hushabye.

Kasper grabbed Hushabye by the hand.

She was dangling in midair.

The stairs had crashed to the ground below.

Smoke was threatening to engulf them.

Kasper fell to his knees, trying to lift Hushabye up.

"Help me!" said Hushabye, in a faint voice.

Kasper held on to her hand as tight as he could. Because of the heat, both of their hands were slippery with sweat. Kasper was beginning to lose his grip.

Also, the few remaining steps where Kasper stood didn't feel too safe. He could hear them creaking and feel them moving beneath him.

He grabbed Hushabye with his other hand and lifted her higher.

She managed to swing her leg up to the nearest step.

Kasper pulled harder and harder.

Finally, with one big heave, Kasper tugged Hushabye up.

"Years of housework have made me very strong," Kasper said.

"Stop boasting!" Hushabye told him.

They rushed up to the top of the steeple.

"Honey!"

"You must be Sister Pumpkin," said Hushabye. "Now, don't worry. We'll soon have you out of there."

"Honey!"

Kasper and Hushabye tried to raise the bell.

It didn't budge.

"We're not going to do it!" gasped Kasper.

"Nonsense, Brother Kasper," said Hushabye. "You give up too easily. On the count of three, we'll both lift for all we're worth. Ready?"

Kasper took a deep breath and nodded.

"Here we go then! One, two, three . . . LIFT!"

Slowly, they lifted the bell enough for Pumpkin to be able to get out.

"Crawl under, Sister Pumpkin!" cried Hushabye, panting for breath.

But Pumpkin didn't move.

She just stared and said, "Honey!"

"She's too scared!" panted Kasper.

The bell started to slip through their fingers.

"Move, Sister Pumpkin!"

Still Pumpkin did nothing except stare and say, "Honey."

"Hold the bell as tight as you can, Brother Kasper!" cried Hushabye. "I'm going to pull Sister Pumpkin out!"

Hushabye got to her knees. She reached under the bell

and grabbed hold of one of Pumpkin's feet. "Come on, Sister Pumpkin!"

Pumpkin didn't move.

Kasper could feel the bell slipping.

"Hurry!" he yelled.

Hushabye pulled Pumpkin's foot.

Slipping.

Hushabye gave Pumpkin's foot an extra-hard tug, and Pumpkin fell to the floor.

"Move, Sister Pumpkin! Move!"

"Hurry!" yelled Kasper.

Hushabye pulled and pulled at Pumpkin's foot. It appeared under the bell. She reached for the other foot and pulled.

"I'm going to drop the bell!" cried Kasper. "It's too heavy."

"A few more seconds, Brother Kasper!" panted Hushabye, pulling both of Pumpkin's feet.

Pumpkin's legs appeared.

Then her waist.

"Hurry!"

Slipping.

Her arms.

Slipping.

Her chest.

Her shoulders.

Her head.

The bell slipped through Kasper's fingers.

Bong!

But Pumpkin was safely out.

Kasper wrapped his arm around Pumpkin and kissed her.

"Oh, Pumpkin!" he cried. "Pumpkin."

"No time for that, Brother Kasper. Look!"

Kasper turned to see—

Flames were now visible where the stairs had been.

"The stairs have gone!" cried Hushabye. "That means—"

"We're trapped!" cried Kasper.

"Trapped!" cried Pumpkin.

"What are we going to do?" cried Hushabye.

"I don't know," admitted Kasper.

"Trapped!" Pumpkin's eyes grew even wider. Now she was too scared to do anything but tremble and murmur "trapped" over and over again.

"Keep calm, Pumpkin."

Flames licked up the stone walls.

Sparks filled the air.

Smoke was everywhere.

"Oh, Brother Kasper . . . I've never been so scared."

Tears trickled down Hushabye's cheeks.

"I'm not crying, Brother Kasper. It's just the smoke making my eyes water."

"Certainly."

Crash!

A large stone fell from the steeple.

It crashed through the floor, narrowly missing Kasper and Hushabye.

"Ahhh!" screamed Hushabye.

"Ahhh!" screamed Kasper.

They rushed into each other's arms and held each other tight.

"Trapped . . ."

More flames.

More sparks.

More smoke.

"What are we going to do, Brother Kasper?"

"We'll think of something—"

Crash!

Another stone fell.

Right through the floor.

Flames appeared in the hole.

"Ahhh!"

"Ahhh!"

"Trapped!"

"Brother Kasper . . . I want you to know . . . just in case we don't get out of this—"

"Don't talk like that, Hushabye—"

"Listen to me, Brother Kasper. I want you to know that your plan was very sensible and it wasn't your fault things went wrong. I hope you know that when I said 'I love you' downstairs, I wasn't looking at King Streetwise. I was looking at you."

"I know that, Hushabye."

"You see, as I told you, I could never lie about something like that—"

Crash!

"Ahhhh!"

"Ahhhh!"

"Trapped!"

Flames!

Sparks!

Smoke!

"Brother . . . Kasper . . ." Hushabye was coughing now. "I also want you to know"—cough!—"you're the best friend I've ever had."

"And you're the best friend I've ever had."

Kasper squeezed Hushabye's hand.

And then he heard the loudest scream he had ever heard.

"AHHHHH!"

It was Pumpkin.

"What is it, Pum—" he began.

And then he realized.

His suit was on fire!

uddenly, Pumpkin was on him. She was slapping at the flames with her bare hands.

"Pumpkin!" cried Kasper.

But she just kept on slapping until the flames were out.

"There!" she said. "You're safe now."

"You're moving, Sister Pumpkin!"

"And about time, too!" Pumpkin said. "What a stupid woman I've been! Not even helping you lift the bell off me! Honestly! Well, I'll make up for it now! I'll help us get out of here. You all right, honey?"

"Y . . . yes."

"Good. Now cover your mouth with your handkerchief so you don't breathe in any smoke. Have you got a hanky, Hushabye?"

"No . . . no, Sister Pumpkin."

"Then here—" Pumpkin said, tearing a piece from her nightdress. "Use this."

"Thank you, Sister Pumpkin."

"Now then," Pumpkin said, tearing another piece from her nightdress to cover her own mouth, "we can't go down the stairs—"

"There are no stairs, Sister Pumpkin."

"Exactly! So then the only way out is through one of these windows!"

"We're a long way up, Sister Pumpkin."

"We've got no choice, Hushabye. And look out! Another piece of stone is falling!"

Kasper and Hushabye moved out of the way.

The stone fell and went straight through the belfry floor.

More flames shot through the hole.

More sparks.

More smoke.

Pumpkin looked out one of the openings and into the street below. "There's Heartthrob wearing the golden cloak," she said.

"No, Pumpkin," corrected Kasper. "It's Streetwise who wears the golden cloak."

"Don't argue, honey," snapped Pumpkin. "I may have looked like a senseless cabbage earlier, but I've been listening to people talking, so I've worked out a few things. And that," she said, pointing, "is most definitely Heartthrob."

Kasper and Hushabye rushed to Pumpkin's side.

"Good heavens!" exclaimed Kasper. "You're right, Pumpkin."

Heartthrob was swishing the golden cloak around and around.

"Brother Heartthrob!" called Hushabye. "What are you

doing with that senseless thing? You look like a Christmas tree!"

Heartthrob looked up and shouted, "Streetwise got away! He ran like a scaredy-cat! But not before I snatched the cloak! And gave him a black eye—"

"Stop boasting and help us!" yelled Pumpkin.

"Righto, Sister Pumpkin! You tell him!"

"Get the Argonauts and Jingo!" Pumpkin called to Heartthrob. "You've got to hold the cloak out so we can—" She broke off, coughing.

The smoke was getting thicker and thicker.

"I know what you're getting at, Sister Pumpkin," said Hushabye. "What a sensible plan. Brother Heartthrob, hold the cloak out with the others. We're going to have to jump into it." Then she broke off, coughing, too.

"But it's too high, man—"

"No buts, Heartthrob," called Kasper.

"But, man—"

"DON'T ARGUE, CHILD!" shouted Pumpkin.

Kasper stared at Pumpkin in amazement. He'd never heard her sound so forceful before.

"Now, as I'm the heaviest," Pumpkin said, "you two go first. I'll need you two to help hold the cloak to support my weight. Hushabye, you jump first."

Hushabye crawled over the edge of the opening.

Crasshh!

Another brick fell.

Fire.

Sparks.

Smoke.

Heartthrob and the others were holding the golden cloak out below now.

"Jump, man."

"Jump, Mistress Hushabye!"

Hushabye took a deep breath and jumped.

"AAIEEYAHH!" went Hushabye.

She landed in the golden cloak, bounced a few times, then clambered off.

"Now you, honey."

"I don't want to go without you, Pumpkin."

"Don't argue—"

"I won't, Pumpkin."

"All right, honey. We'll go together."

They both sat on the edge of the opening and looked down.

"Jump, Brother Kasper! Jump, Sister Pumpkin!"

"Jump, Master Kasper! Jump, Mistress Pumpkin."

"Jump, men."

"Jump, squires."

"Jump, old beans!"

"Jump, chiefs!"

"Woof, mateys!"

Kasper and Pumpkin looked at each other.

Pumpkin held out her hand.

Kasper took it.

They smiled.

And then, hand in hand, they jumped into the gold.

AIEEYAHH!" went Kasper.

"AAIEEYAHH!" went Pumpkin.

They landed in the golden cloak, bounced a few times, then lay there, gasping.

"They're not frazzled, are they, squires?"

"Are they safe, old beans?"

"Tell me they're cool, chiefs!"

"Are they woof, mateys?"

"Don't worry, Brothers. They're just getting their breath back. That's all. Correct, Brother Heartthrob?"

"Spot on, man. They're totally safe."

"Safe as houses, I'd say. Gracious me, yes. Do you need any help, Master Kasper and Mistress Pumpkin?"

"Not at all," replied Pumpkin. "At least, I don't. What about you, honey?"

"Certainly not, Pumpkin."

"Good. Now put the cloak down, everyone, so honey and I can get off. That's it. Goodness! The fire *is* spreading quickly! The whole building'll fall down soon! Look. The steeple's toppling! We should get to the other side of the street as soon as possible. Those who can see will have to help those who can't."

"Very sensible, Sister Pumpkin," said Hushabye. "And here—wear the cloak. Your nightgown won't be warm enough—"

"But *I* want to wear it, man—"

"It's about time this cloak was put to a sensible use, Brother Heartthrob! Or do you want Sister Pumpkin to shiver all night?"

Heartthrob shook his head. "She can wear it," he said softly.

"Here, Sister Pumpkin," said Hushabye, draping the cloak over Pumpkin's shoulders.

"Thank you, Hushabye," said Pumpkin. "Very sensible."

They all rushed to the other side of the street.

They watched the Palace burn for a while, fire blazing in their eyes.

Then . . .

"LISTEN TO ME!" announced Pumpkin. "NOW, YOU ALL KNOW WHO I AM. I'M MY HONEY'S MOTHER. AND YOU KNOW WHAT THAT MEANS? IT MEANS I LOOK AFTER HIM. I KNOW I MIGHT NOT HAVE BEEN THE BEST MOTHER IN THE PAST, BUT THINGS ARE GOING TO CHANGE FROM NOW ON. WHY? BECAUSE I'VE CHANGED. AND I'VE GOT ALL OF YOU TO THANK FOR THAT! THAT'S WHY I WANT YOU ALL TO COME BACK HOME WITH ME. I SUPPOSE THE PLACE IS A WRECK AFTER LAST NIGHT'S ATTACK—BUT IT'S STILL A HOME! PLEASE

LET ME CARE FOR YOU. BECAUSE I DO CARE! WITH ALL MY HEART!"

There was a long pause while everyone thought about what Pumpkin had just said.

Then Knucklehead walked up to Pumpkin and rubbed his head against her legs. "Woof," he said gently.

"Woof to you, Knucklehead," said Pumpkin, stroking his hair.

And, one by one, all the children went to Pumpkin and wrapped their arms around her.

And she embraced them, the sequined cloak engulfing everyone like the wings of some gigantic golden bird.

"Let's go home," said Pumpkin.

And, with that, she led the way down the street.

Kasper looked back at the Palace.

The fire was still burning, illuminating the night sky.

The color?

Golden, of course.

Good heavens! thought Kasper. I don't think I've ever felt so uncomfortable.

He was in his bedroom, trying to get to sleep. Only he wasn't in his bed, as normal. He was on the floor. And he was covered by a tattered sheet. And he wasn't alone. He had Heartthrob, Jingo, Skinnybones, Poodlecut, Finger-poppin, Knucklehead, and Hushabye in the room with him.

Good heavens! thought Kasper. There's not enough room to turn over. And there's a draft coming through the broken window. And Knucklehead's knees are sticking in my back—

And then Pumpkin called out from her bedroom, "Good night, everyone!"

"Good night, man!" replied Heartthrob.

"Good night, Mistress Pumpkin!" replied Jingo.

"Good night, squire!" replied Skinnybones.

"Good night, old bean!" replied Poodlecut.

"Good night, chief!" replied Fingerpoppin.

"Woof, matey!" replied Knucklehead.

"Good night, Sister Pumpkin!" replied Hushabye.

Good heavens! thought Kasper. Pumpkin sounds so happy. She's been like that since we got back to the house. I thought she was going to burst into tears when she saw what a wreck Streetwise had made of the place. But no! She just told everyone to help her tidy the place up. Pumpkin worked the hardest. I'd never seen her do so much housework. Come to think of it, I'd never seen her do *any* housework—

And then Heartthrob called out, "Good night, men!"

"Good night, Master Heartthrob!"

"Good night, squire!"

"Good night, old bean!"

"Good night, chief!"

"Woof, matey!"

"Good night, Brother Heartthrob!"

"Good night, honey!"

Honey! thought Kasper. Pumpkin is calling Heartthrob honey. I'm not sure I like this. I'm supposed to be her only honey. Mind you, I'm not surprised. After cleaning the house, Pumpkin cooked something to eat for everyone. I offered to help. But Pumpkin didn't even answer me. She was too busy talking to the others. In fact, she hardly looked in my direction—

And then Jingo called out, "Good night, Masters and Mistresses!"

"Good night, man!"

"Good night, squire!"

"Good night, old bean!"

"Good night, chief!"

"Woof, matey!"

"Good night, Brother Jingo!"

"Good night, honey!"

Another honey! thought Kasper. Obviously every child in the world is Pumpkin's honey now. *Nothing surprises me anymore.* After eating, Pumpkin told us all to go to bed. And she got sheets out and put everyone in my bedroom! She didn't even ask if I minded or not—

And then Skinnybones called out, "Good night, squires!"

"Good night, man!"

"Good night, Master Skinnybones!"

"Good night, old bean!"

"Good night, chief!"

"Woof matey!"

"Good night, Brother Skinnybones!"

"Good night, honey!"

Good heavens! Now I've got Heartthrob's elbow in my ear! And Skinnybones is sniffing for roses, and Poodlecut is listening for moths. They can't get used to the fact they don't have to frazzle and shoo anymore—

And then Poodlecut called out, "Good night, old beans!"

"Good night, man!"

"Good night, Master Poodlecut!"

"Good night, squire!"

"Good night, chief!"

"Woof, matey!"

"Good night, Brother Poodlecut!"

"Good night, honey!"

Good heavens! I'm never going to get to sleep at this rate! And Pumpkin didn't even blow me a kiss goodnight—

And then Fingerpoppin called out, "Good night, chiefs!"

"Good night, man!"

"Good night, Master Fingerpoppin!"

"Good night, squire!"

"Good night, old bean!"

"Woof, matey!"

"Good night, Brother Fingerpoppin!"

"Good night, honey!"

I've never heard so many voices in the house! I'll never get to sleep at this rate!

And then Knucklehead called out, "Woof, mateys!"

"Good night, man!"

"Good night, Master Knucklehead!"

"Good night, squire!"

"Good night, old bean!"

"Good night, chief!"

"Good night, Brother Knucklehead!"

"Good night, honey!"

No more! thought Kasper. Please—

And then Hushabye called out, "Good night, Brothers and Sister!"

"Good night, man!"

"Good night, Mistress Hushabye!"

"Good night, squire!"

"Good night, old bean!"

"Good night, chief!"

"Woof, matey!"

"Good night, honey!"

Well, I'm not going to say good-night to anyone! I can't be bothered! This is my bedroom, and I can do what I like. And perhaps now that all the good-nighting is over and done with, I can have some peace and quiet—

And that's when the snoring started!

Zzzzz went Heartthrob.

Zzzzz went Jingo.

Zzzzz went Skinnybones.

Zzzzz went Poodlecut.

Zzzzz went Fingerpoppin.

Zz—woof went Knucklehead.

Zzzzz went Hushabye.

And he even heard Pumpkin going *Zzzzz*—instead of "A facial!"—in her bedroom.

Good heavens! This is too much! I'm used to silence and comfort when I sleep. At the moment, I've got neither. And—what's that? Something flashing! Oh, I don't believe it! The sunbed has started flashing on and off downstairs again. And who's going to turn it off? Me, I suppose!

Kasper kicked the sheet from him and went downstairs to the salon.

He went over to the sunbed.

And that's when he heard a noise in the garden.

"Who's there?" demanded Kasper, looking out of the window.

"Well—hey there!—moonlit dude," said a voice from the garden.

STREETWISE!"

"Shush! Don't shout! You'll wake the others! And I don't want that to happen. You look nervous. Well—hey there!—you're not scared of me, are you, moonlit dude?"

"Cer . . . certainly not."

"Because you needn't be. How can I possibly hurt you? Look at me! My once glorious and golden body is scorched and covered in soot. And look what Heartthrob gave me! A black eye. It's so painful. Oh, no, moonlit dude. I'm not here to hurt you. I just want to talk. That's all."

"I don't want to talk to you! You kidnapped my Pumpkin!"

"But I have so many new heartaches—ouch!"

"What . . . sort of new heartaches?"

"I've lost everything, moonlit dude. Everything! And every loss is a heartache. My Palace is gone—ouch! My cloak is gone—ouch! My Argonauts are gone—ouch! Oh, I have more heartaches than there are stars in the sky! But do you know what the brightest star in my constellation of heartaches is?"

"What?"

"You, moonlit dude."

"M . . . me?"

"Of course! From that first moment I saw you and tasted your yummy Banoffi pie, I knew that we were meant to be friends."

"You . . . did?"

"Of course! Can I come closer, moonlit dude?"

"If you want to."

"You won't run away?"

"No."

"Thank you! Well—hey there!—I can see you better now. Oh, look at your hair. It's been burnt. And you're

covered in soot, too. Both of us have seen better days, hey, moonlit dude?"

"Ab . . . absolutely."

"And we'll see them again! Together! Look at the City. Doesn't it look beautiful?"

"It does."

"You liked it in the Gloom, didn't you?"

"Certainly."

"You liked the excitement and the freedom?"

"Y . . . yes."

"You liked all those sights and sounds— Wait! That's not a moth, is it?"

"Just a little one."

"Yuck! Shoo it out of the way for me!"

"Shoo, moth! Shoo! There! It's gone!"

"Thank you, moonlit dude. I'm glad you shooed the moth for me, because it proves one thing."

"What?"

"You still like me."

"Well . . . perhaps."

"And you still want to be my friend, don't you?"

"I . . . I suppose I do."

"So what are you waiting for? In the Gloom you can have everything! Here—in this home—you've got nothing. Pumpkin doesn't need you anymore. You know that. Pumpkin won't have time for you from now on. She's got all the other children. Well, she's welcome to them all. I offered them all my glorious and golden friendship, and they turned their backs on me. But you—you're different, moonlit dude. You're not like the others at all. You're the most special friend I've ever had. You and I can rule the Gloom together. King Streetwise and . . . Prince Kasper!"

"Prince Kasper?"

"You like the sound of it?"

"Certainly."

"Then say you have no home and come with me! Say it, moonlit Prince. Say it and end my many heartaches."

"I . . . I—"

"Say it!"

"I . . ."

"SAY IT!"

"I HAVE NO HOME!"

"You are my Prince! Now climb out the window."

"Certainly."

"Hurry, Prince Kasper of the Gloom—"

*L*EAVE MY SON ALONE!"
cried Pumpkin.

She was standing in the doorway to the salon, draped in the golden cloak, and glaring at Streetwise.

"P . . . P . . . Pumpkin!" stammered Kasper. He was perched across the window ledge, one leg inside the house, one leg outside. "St . . . Streetwise wants me—"

"Of course I want you, moonlit dude. And you want me, don't you? Tell your yucky mother you want me!"

"I . . . I . . ." stammered Kasper.

"He doesn't want you!" cried Pumpkin, marching up to the window and glaring at Streetwise. "He wants me! I'm his mother—"

"Don't listen to her, moonlit dude. She doesn't need you anymore! You don't even call her mother—"

"He can call me mother if he wants to!"

Kasper looked at Pumpkin, then Streetwise, confused.

Streetwise smiled. "Why don't we let the moonlit dude decide for himself?" he hissed. "He can come with me or stay with his yucky mother. What do you want, moonlit dude? I'm offering you the chance to be Prince of the Gloom."

Kasper looked at Streetwise.

"I love you, honey," said Pumpkin.

Kasper looked at Pumpkin.

"Be my friend, moonlit dude," said Streetwise.

Kasper looked at Streetwise.

"I love you, honey."

Kasper looked at Pumpkin.

"Be my friend, moonlit dude. And if you won't be my friend back, I'll tear everything that belongs to you—"

"That's it!" cried Kasper, climbing off the window ledge and into the house. "I know what I want! I want Pumpkin! I remember what you're like now, Streetwise! The truth of it! You can't force people to be your friend! It just happens naturally! Like I love Pumpkin. So go away and leave us alone!"

"Go!" said Pumpkin.

"You yucky—" began Streetwise.

"DO AS YOU'RE TOLD!" yelled Pumpkin. "I'M THE MOTHER AROUND HERE!"

Streetwise glared at Pumpkin for a moment, then backed out of the garden. "One day you'll belong to me," he said, pointing at Kasper. And then he shrieked, "ONE DAY ALL THE CHILDREN OF THE WORLD WILL BELONG TO ME!"

And, with that, Streetwise turned around and ran towards the City.

*H*e's gone," sighed Kasper.

"No, honey, he's not gone. He's out there in the Gloom. And he's going to start rebuilding his Kingdom pretty soon: a new Palace, new Throne, new Chariot . . . and new Argonauts! That's why I've got to help them, honey. All the children. To save them from Streetwise! If they're already in the Gloom and haven't got proper homes, then they've got to be looked after. If they're happy in their homes—then they've got to be warned. Warned that Streetwise is out there, waiting to tempt them away and make them Argonauts! I'm going to make posters. And on them I'll write: BEWARE KING STREETWISE! Oh, honey, what's wrong? You look so sad."

"Wh . . . where do I fit in all this?" asked Kasper. "With so many other children to worry about, you won't need me anymore."

"Honey! How can you say that? I'll always need you. Things will change, yes. But for the better. I love you more now that I've got more things to love. Why, I love you enough to . . . to stop a shooting star."

"I love you enough to stop a shooting star as well, Pumpkin," he said, smiling.

And they hugged each other as tightly as they could.

"What's that, honey? There's something in your pocket!"

"Where?"

"In your breast pocket! I felt it when I hugged you."

Kasper felt in his pocket and found—

"The brooch!" he said. "Look, Pumpkin, it's the brooch! I . . . I must have put it in my pocket when I went to shoo the moth from your nose. And . . . I forgot all about it. Pumpkin, I had it on me all this time. There was never any need for me to go to the City in the first place.

Do you know what that means? None of this need have happened!"

"I know, honey," said Pumpkin, smiling. "But I'm glad it has."

"Me too," said Kasper.

"Now, come on, honey—let's go to bed. Look! The sun's coming up! And we want to get a few hours' sleep at least. We've got a lot of work to do from now on."

"Saving children?"

"That's right, honey," said Pumpkin, taking Kasper's hand and walking towards the stairs. "Just like you saved me."

"But it was you who saved me when my suit was on fire."

"But it was you who saved me when I was trapped under the bell," said Pumpkin, leading Kasper up the stairs.

"But you saved me just now when Streetwise came back to get me."

"I tell you what, honey," said Pumpkin. "Why don't we just say we saved each other."

"Certainly, Mum," said Kasper.